Carrie in the Mirror

Breeanna Greska

BLACK ROSE
writing™

ISBN: 978-1-61296-428-7

PUBLISHED BY BLACK ROSE WRITING

www.blackrosewriting.com

Printed in the United States of America

Suggested retail price $15.95

Carrie in the Mirror is printed in Adobe Caslon Pro

To Joyce, who somehow finds the beauty in everything.

Carrie in the Mirror

Chapter 1

It wasn't an uncommon position to find me in these days. I sat slumped against my desk with my head in my hand, staring out the window, even though there wasn't anything particularly interesting out there. The night was foggy and dark, and a light rain tapped my window, the solid thump of each drop almost comforting to my brooding mood. Almost two hours had gone by since I started my American Literature paper, but all that was written on my computer screen was my name and the date. Instead of working, I'd watched the raindrops hit the window and try to determine which drop would race to the bottom of the pane first. All of my nights were like this.

She'd died about four months ago, but the pain hadn't subsided. Instead, it had morphed into numbness, causing me to experience a lack of emotion and an unwillingness to be active or social. It didn't take long for my once sympathetic peers to gossip about my newfound recklessness and claim that I needed to get over it already. This might be true, but I don't think any of them can understand what it's like to lose an identical twin.

She was beautiful, far more beautiful than me despite our identicalness. Her hair shone just a little bit brighter, as though there had been gold threaded into it, despite our hair being dark. The freckles lightly dusted across her nose were cute, whereas mine were bold and offending. Her smile was mischievous and contagious, and every word that came out of her managed to be both lilting and melodic. The praise she received from our teachers and parents was never-ending, and her humorous and affective personality earned her friends with no problem. I'd only had one real friend, and even he wouldn't speak to me anymore. I'm still trying to come to terms with the fact that it was her and not me.

I can still remember the awe I'd felt at every story she'd share with me before we went to bed. Even though we were seventeen years old, I'd long for our childhood every once in a while. Some nights, I'd pull my mattress into her room and set it up beside her bed, and we'd talk for hours, often surprised at the sight of sunlight creeping through the window. She was a lot braver than me, as her stories about her relationships with boys would reveal. I know that my mother wishes that it had been me.

Mornings used to be our favorite time of the day. I'd wake up, stumble down the stairs and rub my eyes, blindly feeling my way to the table. The aroma of pancakes, bacon and the sweetest scented oranges would activate my senses, awakening me far better than any alarm could. Carrie had no problem waking up, and her alertness and chattiness that I used to find annoying was now something I'd trade my life for just to experience again for five minutes.

Along with my father and my older brother, Andrew, we'd all engage in a humorous banter, and my heart would often swell with love during these moments. After making sure everyone else was served, my mother would sit down with the weird, lopsided pancake and the fatty bacon that no one else wanted. Thinking about this, I wish I could go back and give her the fluffiest pancake. Maybe if she had more fluffy pancakes in her life, she wouldn't be as depressed today.

She'd beam at everyone, chiming in to talk about how proud she was, or reminding us that she'd tossed an extra cookie into our lunches. The smiles she once gave me would light up the sky like the finale in a fireworks show. Now, after Carrie, the most I receive from her is a scowl, a welcome improvement from the blank stare that constantly occupies her face. When I go down to the kitchen in the morning, the sunny yellow aura that previously occupied the room has now been replaced by a dull, misty grey. Instead of sitting down to sweet waffles drenched in syrup, I lifelessly pour cold cereal into a bowl, only to realize that the milk in the refrigerator has expired. Again.

Things in this house have changed immensely since Carrie.

Groceries are only picked up about once a month, if at all, and it usually only consists of a few microwavable meals, milk, which goes rotten, bread, which goes stale, and eggs, which tend to stay in the back of the refrigerator untouched. My mother has dropped in weight and the glow that used to cover her entire face was now replaced by a sickly pale color, almost as if she'd dumped a pound of flour on her face. Her once healthy looking limbs were now frail and untouchable, which was difficult for me to deal with, because sometimes, I just wanted someone to hold me. She no longer wanted that job, and that was something that I couldn't concede.

Dust piled up behind the refrigerator, which was unfortunate, because I kind of didn't like having a cloud of particles burst out at me every time I opened the door. Most people might be used to having dust in hard to reach places, but Mom used to be a clean-freak. She'd gather her supplies every Saturday and hum while she scrubbed and scoured every inch of the house. It was weird to see a sink that was once sparkling now covered in the beginnings of rust.

The garden in our front yard used to win contests. The vibrant colors of the delicate flowers, the size and obvious life of the trees and plants, and the abundance of butterflies that collected themselves in the vicinity made our garden the most beautiful and inviting one in the neighborhood. The refrigerator used to hold clippings of Mom's prizewinning picture, her grin so wide it was almost manic. Carrie would be on her left and I'd be on her right, our arms stretched across her back, our freckles highlighted in the sun. We'd each hold up a huge Scarlet Pimpernel, its deep blue color almost identical to our eyes. The refrigerator was now dingy and bare.

Chapter 2

I attempted to rouse myself from this nostalgic daydream, because it never did me any good. I glanced at the computer screen and remembered that I'd been typing a paper. Well, I'd been trying to type a paper. My teachers were used to receiving my papers late or not receiving them at all. At first, they'd been sympathetic and sensitive, allowing me to turn in work without penalty. Now, they'd become frustrated and hopeless, expecting the same work I'd done before. I used to cry if I'd get a B. I was probably the most diligent, attentive student anyone could ever meet. I remember getting my report cards back and letting out a squeal of delight when seeing the perfect row of A's beaming back at me. They were so alive in that moment that I genuinely viewed them as smiling, congratulatory beings. I'd race home and run to show my father, who would swoop me up in his arms and plant a kiss on my forehead, eyes crinkling as he'd tease me for being a nerd. We'd always go out to an old-fashioned sweets shop downtown, just me and him. I can still taste the sundae I'd get every time. The creamy mint chocolate-chip was always sweet and cold, and I'd top it with hot fudge, whipped cream, pecans and two cherries, one of which Dad would always try to steal. I'd defensively jab my spoon in his direction, and then burst into a fit of giggles because he'd tickle me to dodge my attempted stabbing.

Shaking my head, I stood up and stretched, slipping into an old grey jacket. I quietly made my way over to my bedroom door, begging it not to create the squeaks or groans the old house was prone to when I opened it. I stealthily crept across the hallway, shuffling down the stairs in my socks in an attempt to keep from waking my parents. As I came to the front door, I was met with a shadow and realized that there was a figure in my kitchen. I grabbed an umbrella that was on top of the end table in the foyer, although I wasn't sure what good that would do. I began to tiptoe toward the kitchen when I heard soft sobbing coming from the figure, whose shoulders were shaking uncontrollably. Taking a step back, I realized it was my father.

My father never cried. Even at my Papa's funeral, he'd stood tall next to the casket, putting on a gracious smile when guests stopped to console him. Instead of giving hugs, he'd firmly shake their hands. At Carrie's funeral, Dad had to be the strong one. Mom was completely out of commission, so the job was passed to him without consent. He'd somehow managed to be on a far more balanced and controlled level than the rest of us, and I don't recall his grief as something that was overly visible. This was strange to me, and I wasn't sure what to make of it. Watching my father, I struggled to hold back the tears that were desperately trying to make their way out of my eyes.

It was so hard to come to terms with what this family had become. I wanted to be there for my parents, but they wouldn't let me. Sometimes I'd curse my appearance, curse the fact that I ever even had an identical twin. It hurt my mother to look at me, and when she did look at me, she wanted me to be someone else.

I knew my dad wouldn't even notice if I left, so I flipped my hood over my head and quietly closed the door. The rain had stopped for the most part, but the air was brisk and harsh, so I wrapped my jacket around myself tightly. The crunching of the leaves beneath my feet seemed incredibly loud today, but I was thankful for them, because they blocked out my thoughts. I always walked at a very quick pace. Carrie used to tell me that I walked with such purpose that she believed I was on a mission. The neighborhood was eerily quiet, and only some of the streetlights worked, shrouding everything that was once familiar to me in a cloud of darkness. It wasn't easy to stop the memories that came flooding into my mind.

I passed the corner store, which was technically named Friendly Foods, but Carrie and I always called it "Irma's," after the woman that owned it, a sweet grandmotherly figure that all the neighborhood children looked up to. In the summer, we'd always flock to the store for the homemade strawberry ice pops she'd make, bursting with real strawberries that she grew in her garden. Carrie was obsessed with strawberries, and begged our parents to let us grow a strawberry patch, promising that she'd take care of it. Of course, the patch was a goner within the first few years, but it was nice to have for a while.

I could barely feel the light mist of rain as I passed the supposedly haunted house a few blocks further. A very old woman lived there, and she'd been there for what seemed like forever, even when our parents were children. Everyone referred to her as "Old Lady Hild," and it was common knowledge that she was a witch. One Halloween, Carrie had been a princess, and I'd been a fairy. I remember her begging me to be the dragon that kidnapped the princess, and I refused, angered at her jealousy and demand to have the prettiest costume. We'd been heading home, comparing and trading candy. I was a big fan of anything chocolate while she loved fruit-flavored and hard candy.

Black-clad teenagers had appeared out of nowhere, clutching eggs, toilet paper, and shaving cream to their chests, clearly ready to riot. Carrie had pulled me into the bushes, which unfortunately happened to be in Old Lady Hild's yard. I was terrified and my heart was beating so furiously that I was surprised the teenagers hadn't heard it and dragged us out. Carrie, however, wonderful Carrie, had whispered Old Lady Hild jokes into my ear and held my hand. I thought a sufficient amount of time had passed when we saw a flash of white hair in the window. We both let out bloodcurdling screams, bolted from the bushes, and ran like our lives depended on it. It had taken at least ten minutes to catch our breaths. Times that I completely took for granted were times that I now spent hours going over, trying desperately to remember each and every detail, wishing I could capture it in a jar and take it out whenever I wanted to, but I had to come to terms with the fact that I couldn't.

Chapter 3

Carrie had died in a car accident. Armed with her newly acquired license and a sleek pair of designer sunglasses, it seemed that she never tired of driving. If one of my parents asked one of us to get something from the store, she'd instantly jump up and volunteer, eager to drive through the neighborhood with the music blaring and the windows rolled down. Her long hair would be streaming out behind her shoulders from the wind, her face cool and composed, like someone who'd been born to drive. Although it seemed like half the time she'd drive simply to show off, she was still a good driver. She'd passed her test with a waiver and obeyed all traffic laws at all times, so the accident came as a huge surprise to my family.

We'd been watching a hockey game in the living room when the call came. My dad, who just moments before had been yelling at the TV and pumping his fist in the air, became a sickly shade of white after he answered the phone. He dropped the remote and began clutching at his chest, moving his mouth without really speaking. My mother ran over to him, screaming at him to tell her what was going on, and my brother and I sat there in fear, having never seen our parents react at anything like this.

The officers said that Carrie had been going the speed limit and were still struggling to figure out why she'd hit the other car the way she did. She hadn't died immediately, and we all rushed to the hospital to see her, each of us holding on for hope, especially since the officers had explained that the accident didn't seem fatal.

By the time we reached the hospital, we were greeted by a doctor who looked far too young to be telling us such grave news. He'd been handsome and charming, trying to put us at ease with his bright smile and easy voice, but it didn't work. My mother had dropped to her knees in the middle of the hospital, repeating over and over that it couldn't be true. My parents both started blaming themselves, agreeing that it was their fault for letting her drive at all. My brother and I were quick to protest them, but neither of us felt much like comforting them when we needed our own comfort. Suddenly, the roles between parents and children reversed.

I had been walking for nearly twenty minutes when a pair of intense, bright headlights shone directly into my face, forcing me to squint my eyes and slow my pace. The car was large and old, and I couldn't make out who was in it from where I stood. As it neared, it suddenly squealed to a stop, and a teenage boy lazily leaned out the window, a grin slowly spreading over his lips.

"Hey there, beautiful," he called, which was interrupted by a flurry of snickers from the passengers in the car. I kept walking, knowing better than to waste my time on such idiots.

"Hey!" the driver yelled. "He's talking to you! It's impolite not to answer!"

I knew it'd be a mistake, but I glanced briefly at the car, which gave me a view of who was in the backseat. My greatest bully, Allison Green. At close to six feet tall, she towered over me physically, and it was her belief that she towered over me mentally as well. Despite my many failed efforts to be polite and respectful to her, she consistently went out of her way to insult me, to do whatever she could to hurt me. I'd never let her see it, but once I was out of her sight, the tears would slowly build up in my eyes, trickling down onto my cheeks, causing my vision to go blurry. I didn't know the exact reason she disliked me so much, and I'm sure I'd never get an answer. What I did know was that I was much smarter than her, and that my attempts to be the better person would one day be rewarded while her constant bullying would be repaid with some bad karma.

"Hey, poor little depressed girl," Allison called mockingly, a wicked glint in her eye. Her short, thin red hair was pulled back in a ponytail, and she was dressed in her usual uniform of sweatpants and a pullover.

I'm no fashion expert, but I definitely do not see the appeal of wearing sweats every single day. She stared at me, her eyes narrowing as she sized me up, lips pursing and clear disdain in her demeanor. I ignored her and kept walking, feeling the pain tugging at my heart but refusing to acknowledge it.

"I'm talking to you!" she shouted, her voice harsh and direct. "Just because your sister died doesn't mean you can treat everyone else like they're scum. You're scum too!"

I clenched my fists, squeezing my fingers together as tightly as possible in an effort to keep the tears from spilling out of my eyes. My face grew hot and blotchy red patches began to sprout in various places. The laughter of everyone in the car seemed to grow louder, taunting me, and my chest felt tight. Suddenly, I heard the sickening crunch of something hitting metal followed by the squeal of tires. I whipped my head around and widened my eyes, surprised to find my old best friend standing defiantly a few feet from the car. A large, lone rock rolled in the street.

"You idiot! You better run, boy! I'll give you a two second head-start, and then I'm going to kick your ass!"

Julian stood there a minute longer, his eyes traveling across the car until they met mine, burning and full of hurt. He turned on his heel and took off through the fog, disappearing almost instantly.

"Freak!" I heard, as Allison tossed a soda can out the window, which promptly ricocheted off of my head. The car sped off, the bass of the music beating at the same rate as my heart. My stomach turned and I suddenly couldn't swallow.

Chapter 4

Julian. He'd been my best friend since we were about eleven years old. I can still remember the day we made the switch to middle school. Carrie, in her neatly coordinated outfit of a pink cardigan, dark rinse jeans, and black ballet flats, was instantly swarmed by all of the girls who'd been considered cool in elementary school. She'd coolly swiped a glittering lip gloss tube across her lips and raised her eyebrow before walking forward with her many fans trailing behind her. I know Carrie was excited at the prospect of becoming a social phenomenon, but I was a little hurt that she'd just left me behind like that.

I bit my lip and anxiously glanced around the wide, unfamiliar hallway, clutching my books and schedule to my chest. I'd opted for a neutral look, wearing a forest green sweater, jeans, and a pair of sneakers, but apparently, casual wasn't in. I almost felt like a victim, my eyes darting around worriedly in every direction, my body stiff and unnaturally balanced against a locker.

"Hi," a voice quietly said behind me. I turned around and came face to face with a boy who was unusually tall for sixth grade. His eyes were dark and brooding, framed by long lashes, slightly slanted and beautiful. His messy, longish black hair tumbled into his eyes, a contrast to his clear, pale skin. He looked like no one I'd ever seen before, and I was instantly drawn to him, glad to see a friendly face. He'd worn heavy black boots, a black long-sleeved shirt and fitted black pants, a far cry from the common jeans, hoodie, and sneaker variety I'd seen around school. He was unusual and different, and I liked it.

"Hey," I answered shyly, unsure of where the conversation was headed.

"I'm headed over to the gym. You going that way?" he'd asked. I had to struggle to hear him, at first assuming that his quiet, gentle tone was the result of shyness on the first day. However, I'd soon grow to learn that Julian always spoke quietly. I sometimes had to strain to listen to what he was saying, but it was always worth it. I glanced down at my schedule, in disbelief when I saw that I had PE first period as well.

"Um, yeah," I said a bit awkwardly, unable to stop from biting my nails.

"Cool. We can walk down there together," he'd said, and without waiting for an answer, began the trek down the hallway.

Brought back to reality, I realized that I'd nearly walked all the way home, almost on autopilot. The shrill shriek of the wind picked up, a haunting background melody to my melancholy thoughts. I picked up the pace, shivering in my jacket. My shoes were nearly soaked through from splashing through the puddles, which had left dark, wet spots on my jeans all the way up to my knees.

I couldn't stop worrying about Julian, wondering why he'd stepped in and where he'd run off to. I wanted badly to call him, but I knew that it was just impossible. I finally reached my walkway and began making my way to the door when I was cut off by a large black cat. I groaned inwardly, yet it wasn't much of a surprise. Of course something like this would happen to me. Bad luck tended to follow me wherever I went. The cat's green eyes flashed at me in annoyance for interrupting his roaming, and I stuck my tongue out at him before hurrying up the stairs. I quietly opened the door and kicked my shoes into the corner, not worried about the mud that would inevitably get on the floor. Months ago, I'd have taken my shoes off outdoors and wiped them off with the rag Mom kept outside before even daring to enter the house. Now, it just didn't matter.

I slid over to the kitchen in my slightly damp socks, flicking on the light. My dad had clearly gone to bed. I hadn't eaten anything that day, so I was feeling a bit hungry. I opened the refrigerator, unsurprised at its weak contents. There was a half-empty bottle of ketchup, some mustard packets from a fast food restaurant that must have been a couple years old, about a third of an onion, wilted lettuce, and some bologna. Grimacing, I headed to the pantry, only to find some canned vegetables that were past their expiration dates. Funny. I thought those things never expired.

I sighed and flipped open the bread compartment, taking out a loaf that felt a little hard. There was nothing much I could do, so I hastily threw a couple slices of bologna, a few leaves of lettuce (trying to avoid any brown parts), and some sliced onions on the bread. Gourmet indeed. I cringed as I took a bite of the stale bread, the flavors leaving an awful, lingering taste in my mouth. I couldn't finish it, so I tossed it in the garbage and decided to call it a night.

My head suddenly started to feel a bit dizzy as I slowly climbed the stairs, and I had to grip the rail before I was able to continue. Ever since Carrie died, these odd little headaches happened a lot. I often wondered if it was her way of still being able to annoy me from wherever she was. I smiled a little to myself, missing all of her silly antics. After brushing my teeth and washing my face, I jumped onto my bed and threw the covers over my head.

It was quite late now, but I still couldn't fall asleep. After tossing and turning for a while, I rolled to the edge of my bed and leaned over to retrieve the box I kept hidden underneath. It contained Carrie's diary. I knew that it was wrong to invade her personal thoughts, but it was one of the things that kept me close to her. I opened it to the page I'd left off at, sliding my fingers across her girly, loopy handwriting. Just reading her thoughts, which were written exactly as she spoke, caused me to break down every time.

A single tear fell onto the page and started to blur the writing. Angry at myself for destroying all that I had left of her, I desperately blew on the page in a mad attempt to revoke my mistake, but my frustration only caused new hot tears to develop. I slammed the diary closed and shoved it under the bed again. My face grew hot, yet I shivered in my oversized sweatshirt, and cried and rocked myself to sleep.

Chapter 5

The next day, I woke up with my hands clutching my stomach. I often slept that way because the nerves that jumbled around wouldn't allow me to sleep, and putting pressure on the area was the only way I'd find stillness. Instead of the rain that had refused to cease yesterday, a ray of warm, incredibly bright sun streamed through my window. I glared at it, angry that the weather no longer matched my mood.

Stomping to my drawer, I pulled out an oversized olive green sweater and tugged on an old pair of jeans. I raked a brush through my thick, tangled hair and rubbed some moisturizer on my skin. Frowning at myself in the mirror, I brushed a little bronzer over my pasty skin and applied some mascara to my lashes. I still looked far from presentable, but as least it was effort. I glanced at the clock in the corner of the room and realized that I was going to be late.

I shoved my feet in a pair of moccasins, slung my backpack over my shoulder and raced down the stairs before skidding into the kitchen. I thought about taking a bagel to go before I remembered that the refrigerator contained absolutely nothing. My stomach growled in protest, especially as this was going on the third day in a row that I'd basically starved myself. I jotted a quick note on a pad of paper on the counter, hoping one of my parents would see it but knowing that it'd be up to me to buy food. I sighed and headed out the door, staring at the jagged cracks in the sidewalk as I made my way toward the school.

As I neared the front, I heard the bell ring. Muttering to myself, I picked up speed and ran for the door, only to be met by Allison.

"Hey, freak," she sneered, glancing down at me and giving me a once-over. Apparently, I failed her test, because she wrinkled her nose and looked at me as though I were a piece of litter on the floor. I ignored her and tried to open the door, but she stuck her foot in my way.

"You know, it hurts my feeling when you don't talk to me," she said, pretending to pout. She twirled her hair and fluttered her eyelashes, putting on an innocent face and waiting expectantly for my answer. I don't know what she wanted me to say, but I'd had about enough of her. I stared at her in her navy blue sweatpants and giant pullover, her freckles menacing and angry as her sharp, dark eyes. I knew I'd probably regret it later, but for now, I just didn't care. I lifted my heavy history book in the air and "accidentally" dropped it on her big toe.

"Oops!" I said sweetly. She jumped back in surprise, swearing loudly before she grabbed her foot and howled. Not wanting to find out what would happen, I grabbed the handle of the door and ran inside without looking back. I felt victory for a brief moment.

The day went by in a blur, as it always seemed to these days. Even though it felt like I'd been in school forever, at the end of the day, I never remembered anything. I knew for certain that I'd received disapproving looks from my teachers, and there were doubtlessly assignments that I'd forgotten to turn in, but other than that, my memory escaped me. I was wary of seeing Allison after school, but all I wanted to do was stop by the store and pick up some frozen dinners. Maybe that'd give me enough energy to finally finish the paper I'd been working on.

I hurriedly walked to the bus stop, glancing over my shoulder every so often in fear that she'd be following me. I rocked back and forth on my heels as I waited, willing the bus to appear. Just as her loud, annoying cackle filled the air (wicked witch indeed), I heard the heavy humming of the bus start to pull up. My heart pounding, I looked behind me. Her eyes flashed and she pointed at me, a wicked smile on her face. She drew her finger across her neck, the universal symbol for "you're dead." I shook my head and stepped on the bus, refusing to acknowledge her childish behavior. That only lasted so long until I had the urge to turn around and shoot her a bright smile. I waggled my fingers and her face was livid. Score.

I was a little nervous to go to the grocery store since Julian worked there. I was hoping that since I'd taken the bus, I would get there and be out before his shift started. When the bus let me out, I conspicuously glanced around the parking lot, hoping I wouldn't see his black car. The coast looked clear, so I rushed to the doors and headed straight for the frozen aisle after grabbing a basket. I mindlessly tossed some boxes in the basket, knowing my limited choices included macaroni and cheese, some sort of pasta, or a chicken dinner. Instead of dreaming about how delicious these meals would taste, especially compared to the makeshift sandwich I'd tried to eat yesterday, my mind was occupied with Julian.

Chapter 6

I couldn't understand why he'd stepped in last night. I can still remember the last time we'd truly talked. It'd been right after Carrie died, and I needed to get out of the house. It had been pouring outside, but I couldn't feel a thing. My hair clung to my face, rain droplets dripping down my chin and sliding into my mouth, but I couldn't taste anything. I felt numb, but for some reason, it felt better than sitting inside my silent house. As I reached the park, a familiar car drove past, but it slowed, and I could see the driver look out the window, concern filling his face.

"Felicia!" he called, in his voice managing to be both deep and lilting. "What are you doing? It's freezing out here! Get in the car!"

I kept walking, unable to concentrate on anything but the sound of the rain hitting the ground. He called my name again, and a twinge of guilt hit me, so I glanced at the car.

"I'm fine," I answered weakly, wanting nothing more than to be alone and hoping he would go away. He didn't get the hint and pulled over, slamming the door and running over to me. He grabbed me by the arm and stared down at me, his brow wrinkled in confusion. He swallowed, almost as if he could sense my pain, and reached out to brush a wet, stringy lock of hair out of my eyes.

"Felicia, what are you doing? You're going to get sick. Just get in the car and let me take you home. We can talk, and I'll make you something to eat. We could watch a movie or something," Julian said, his voice taking on a tone of desperation. I didn't answer, staring blankly ahead and wishing that he'd leave already. Tired of being ignored, he shook my shoulders a little, angry, but still completely concerned.

"Why aren't you talking to me? What's going on with you? I want to be here for you, so why aren't you letting me?"

At the time, I was incredibly selfish, angry at Carrie for leaving, angry at my parents for abandoning me, and angry at the world for turning my life around. I regretted it later, but in that instant, my tantrum felt great and powerful.

"Go away!" I screamed, yanking my shoulder away from his hands and looking straight into his eyes. I was shocked at how hurt he'd appeared, his dark eyes flashing before me, his skin pale and his shoulders seeming to shrink inside of his leather jacket. He'd taken a step back, but didn't leave, waiting for me to come to my senses and get in the car. That wasn't going to happen.

"Why won't you leave me alone?" I continued, my voice high and angry. "You've been following me around like a puppy for the entire week and I'm sick of it! My sister is dead! There's nothing you can do about it! Stop feeling like you need to prove yourself as a friend to me! If you wanted to be a friend, you'd get the hell away from me. The last thing I need right now is you constantly in my face, asking me if I'm okay. I'm not. Alright? So just go away. God!"

The disbelief in his face was incredible, and he gave me one last look filled with pain before he'd turned and slowly walked back to his car, tearing away from the curb as if his life depended on it. I'd sat down shakily, not caring that I'd basically placed myself in a giant puddle. I stayed there nearly the whole night, the wind howling and leaves and twigs flying past me, somehow feeling comfortable in the icy, hard rain.

I was roused from my flashback when I bumped into something, unaware that I'd even stepped away from the freezer. Predictable as it was, of course I'd run into Julian. My life fell somewhere between a cheesy Lifetime movie and a bad teenage comedy. I looked up, my face burning. His dark hair curled under his ears and fell into his eyes, messy in a rock-star kind of way. His eyes, shifting between brown, hazel, and nearly black were curious but suspicious, not unkind, but not quite welcoming. He bit his curved lip, and took a step back, looking as though he wanted to say something, but he remained silent.

"Sorry!" I stammered, overly aware of the awkwardness that hung in the air. Underneath his bright red apron, he wore a black button down shirt, and on top of the shirt, he had on a necklace made from a leather cord that had a single blue and black feather on it. My heart swelled for a moment, knowing that he still wore the necklace I'd made him. Then I remembered the way I'd treated him, and my cheeks burned with shame. He towered over me, making me feel small and insignificant. I couldn't stay there a second longer.

"I've um, got to go," I said quietly, turning quickly on my heels and stumbling over my shoelace, practically running towards the registers.

"Felicia!" I heard. I wanted to look back, but I couldn't face him with the knowledge of how much pain I'd caused him and how he'd still managed to stick up for me. I ducked behind the last register, quickly throwing my items onto the conveyor belt and willing the bored-looking cashier to ring my items a little more quickly.

"Um, seven dollars and fifty cents," she said flatly, rolling her eyes as I dug through my backpack. I pressed a folded ten dollar bill into her hand and grabbed the plastic bags, nearly yanking the change out of her hand as I sprinted to the door.

Chapter 7

When I finally made it home, I immediately put one of the frozen dinners in the microwave, but my mind was preoccupied with Julian. I hoped that would change after I'd eaten. Maybe filling my stomach would empty my mind.

While the dinner cooked, I rooted through my backpack and pulled out a book, hoping to distract myself. It did the trick for a short while. I managed to motivate myself enough to write another two pages of my paper, and then I decided to go to bed. After brushing my teeth and rinsing my face, I put on some old sweatpants and a holey sweater before climbing into bed. I wanted to talk to Carrie, so I reached under the bed and pulled out her diary. Finally, I'd be reaching entries written about a year before she'd died. Although I knew it would hurt to read it, because it was so recent, it made me feel closer to her.

I read until my eyes began to feel heavy, and could feel myself dozing off to sleep. Suddenly, the words on the page startled me, and I sat up, instantly feeling more awake.

Today was such a horrible day. We were all in the locker room after practice, and everyone was changing. We'd been sitting there joking around for a bit and combing our hair when I began changing my shirt. "Getting a little chubby there, are we, Carrie?" I couldn't believe Tara said that! Immediately after, the other girls all started laughing and pinching my stomach, jokingly saying things like, "Peter will be happy. More to love!" I'd never been more mortified. Hearing their statements made me realize I needed to change. From now on, I will be eating absolutely no junk food! No cookies, soda, ice cream, fast food, or potato chips. Instead, I'll only eat fruits, vegetables, and crackers. I'll show them. I have to stay on top...if I don't, my life is going to be ruined. I'm going to go take a jog around the neighborhood to clear my head. Starting now, I'm going to record everything I eat in here, and maybe I'll be able to stop looking like a fat pig.

My fingers started shaking as I struggled to hold the diary up. I squeezed my hands into fists, angry that Carrie's so-called friends had made her feel so horrible. Julian would never do that to me. Great. Now I was back to thinking about Julian.

I carefully placed the diary back into the box and turned my light off, laying my head on my pillow. My mind wandered, picturing Carrie right before she'd died. I knew that she'd been in the hospital, and she'd been incredibly sick and thin, but I didn't ask too many questions. At that moment, I felt like a horrible sister. How could I have not been by her side every moment she'd been in the hospital? I shut my eyes, trying hard to hold back the tears. Even though she'd been very thin before she died, she was so beautiful, and everyone knew it.

As I tossed and turned, I couldn't stop thinking about the diary entry I'd read. Carrie was pretty, smart, and very outgoing. Maybe if I looked more like Carrie, and acted more like Carrie, my mother would have a reason to talk to me again. Maybe I'd make more friends at school. I could even start hanging out with Julian again. For a minute, my heart raced with excitement at the thought of all that could be possible if I made the positive changes Carrie had. Then my heart sunk with the realization that no matter what I did, I'd never be like Carrie.

That night, I had incredibly weird dreams. In one, a frail girl came up to me and grabbed my hand, pressing an apple into it and begging me not to give up. In another, I chased Julian, who kept yelling at me to leave him alone. In the last, Carrie and I were in the rain, yelling at each other. We were wearing the same clothing, and as we started grabbing each other, we morphed into one person. I woke up in a sweat, grabbing the bottle of water I kept by my bedside and chugging it down, confused by my nightmares. I woke up before my alarm went off, so I had time to take a shower.

I remembered my vow to be more like Carrie and turned my

curling iron on. She'd never leave the house without looking perfect. I combed my bangs so they were side-swept and curled my long, dark hair at the ends so gentle ringlets would tumble down my back. Sifting through my closet, I settled on a black and white striped V-neck shirt and black pants, which I paired with grey sandals. Pondering my dreams, I'd come to the conclusion that I needed to bring a bit of Carrie into other people's lives, and the only way I could do that was to try to start living again, even if I needed to take it slow. Maybe, I reasoned with myself, if I brought some kind of life to this house, the atmosphere would change. I actually smiled at myself in the mirror before slipping my hooded windbreaker on.

Chapter 8

Downstairs, I took a frozen breakfast sandwich out of the freezer and heated it in the microwave while drinking a glass of water. I leaned against the counter and picked up the book I'd left there last night.

"Good morning, Felicia," a deep voice rumbled, coughing. I looked up, startled to see my father standing in the kitchen in a black suit. He was never home at the time I left for school. He looked thin and haggard, his thick, dark hair in need of a cut and his blue eyes bloodshot and weary. He walked over to the refrigerator and peered inside for a minute before closing it.

"Guess we should probably buy some groceries, huh?" he asked a little awkwardly, wringing his hands.

"Um, yeah, Dad. We didn't have much. I got some frozen food if you're hungry. It's really great. I mean, it's not great, but if you're hungry, it hits the spot," I babbled, desperately trying to fill the silence and keep my father in the room. He nodded absentmindedly at me and opened the freezer door before shutting it again.

The ringing of a phone startled both of us. My father patted his pockets, a bit lost before he finally located the device. He took it out and glanced at the number, and a strange look crossed his face. He quickly stuffed the phone back in his pocket and grabbed his briefcase, awkwardly clearing his throat.

"Well then," he began, seeming anxious to leave, "I've got to get back to the office. Can you, uh, tell your mother that I won't be back for dinner?" He briskly walked out of the room, and the door slammed.

"What dinner?" I questioned the empty room. I shrugged, a bit put off by the conversation we'd just had, but remembered that everything was weird in this house nowadays. Andrew was so lucky. He was away at school, studying business. At least he got full meals, good friends, and a reason to keep going. I decided to call him later and see how he was doing. He hadn't been home since Christmas, which was far from jolly and painful to endure. I can still recall the weird, lonely day.

I'd woken up around eleven, which is the latest I'd ever slept on Christmas in my entire life. Usually, Carrie would have jumped on my bed with a burst of energy that usually wasn't reserved for six in the morning, shaking me awake with a mischievous grin on her face. I'd throw a pillow over my face and mumble at her to go away, but she'd just rip the blankets off my bed and head to Andrew's room, making sure he was awake too.

This year, however, the house was silent. I was used to waking up to various scents traveling from the kitchen throughout the rest of the house, ranging from the peppermint candles my mother kept lit in the living room to the roasting turkey in the oven. That day, I smelled nothing that was reminiscent of Christmas. I'd walked downstairs to be greeted by a bare living room, the area where the tree usually went sadly vacant. I figured that no one would get up for the rest of the day, and I was right. Instead of indulging in a three course dinner that would be followed by pies, cookies, and hot chocolate, I sat on the couch, Christmas specials playing on the television. I stared at the screen blankly, and soon Andrew joined me, but not a word passed between us.

I sighed as I remembered that awful day, and hoped that maybe things would get a little better by Easter. Slinging my backpack over my shoulder, I took one last bite out of my sandwich and left the house. Since I'd woken early, I took my time walking to school, hoping that the effort I'd put into my hair wouldn't turn into a frizzy mess. For once, I welcomed the warm blanket of sun on my skin, and the slight joy I felt in looking at the flowers that were starting to bloom began to give me hope.

"I'm doing this for you, Carrie," I whispered, instinctively speaking to the sky.

"Oh, talking to yourself again, freak?" a nasal voice whined. I froze in place, realizing that Allison was behind me. I tried to turn around, but I couldn't. I didn't have to, though, because she waltzed up, looking down at me with a manic grin on her face. I stared back at her, and a small chuckle escaped me when I remembered a silly observation Julian had once made. We'd been in the cafeteria and Allison was sitting at the next table, shooting us death glares every now and then. Julian had widened his eyes at her every time, scrunching up his face and wriggling his eyebrows, doing anything he could to annoy her.

"You know," he'd pointed out, "If you connect her freckles, I seriously think they make the face of David Hasslehoff." We'd both burst out laughing, much to the vexation of a miffed Allison.

This time, however, laughing was clearly not a good idea. Her eyes narrowed in anger.

"Who," she hissed, "do you think you are? You thought you were clever yesterday, didn't you? Think I'd just forget it? Think again!"

She laughed wickedly, a glint of menace in her eyes, and wrapped her meaty hand around my arm so I couldn't escape. I couldn't speak, audibly swallowing in fear. She reached into her backpack and pulled out a sealed container, which contained a vile looking green liquid. I knew it was going to happen before it did, but even with all my concentration, I couldn't make myself move. She paused for effect, pouting her lips as if she didn't want to but had no other choice before promptly dumping the entire container on my head.

"Guess we'll think twice next time before deciding to mess with me, okay?" she said, her voice dripping honey sarcasm. "Bow down to your superior!" She turned on her heel and let out a hoot of laughter as she walked away.

So much for trying to make a fresh start. I pulled a hooded sweatshirt from my backpack and carefully wiped my face and hair. Today was the deadline for my literature paper, and I knew that I had to go to school. There was nothing I could do to make myself appear more presentable, so I stuck my hair in a low ponytail and spritzed myself with perfume I kept in my backpack pocket. As I entered the school, I walked quickly to my locker, keeping my head down. Even without looking, I could feel all eyes on me and hear countless snickers. *What would Carrie do? Be like Carrie,* I thought to myself. I sucked in my breath and marched to my locker, flinging it open and turning around to stare down everyone who chose to look my way. I heard some mumbling and giggling, but eventually they looked away.

Most of the day went by in a hazy blur. By the time gym rolled around, I was exhausted. As usual, I was the one of the last ones left to change in the locker room. Today was different for some reason. Instead of avoiding eye contact with everyone and struggling to change behind my locker door, I let my eyes travel. I found myself staring at everyone's legs, noticing the different sizes and colors. I felt slightly ashamed at the wave of emotion that came over me, especially as I have no idea where it came from, but I couldn't stop it.

I found myself repulsed by the thick, flabby limbs that stood solidly encased in red gym shorts. I couldn't believe that I'd never before noticed the dimpled thighs and loose, fleshy arms wobbling as girls slammed their locker doors shut. When everyone had left, I walked to the tall mirror in the center of the locker room. For the first time in months, I really focused on my reflection. My hair had grown longer, but the ends were badly in need of a trim. My skin had become blotchy, its creaminess replaced by harsh, random red marks. The circles under my eyes were dark purple, and my skin color had taken on a yellowish tint. The worst part was my legs.

I'd never worried about them much before, as I always figured I was average, which suited me just fine. Today, they looked like two tree trunks rooted to the ground. Instead of the svelte, lean limbs Carrie had, mine were wide and devoid of muscle. *When had I become this big?* I wondered to myself. Maybe it was the frozen dinners I'd been devouring. Whatever the case, there was no way I could be like Carrie carrying around this amount of weight. I heard the final gym whistle blow and knew I had to hustle out of there. I gave myself one last frown in the mirror and decided to jog to the gym rather than walk at my usual slow, trudging pace. It had to count for something, right?

31

Chapter 9

Later, when I was walking home, I passed over a drawn hopscotch game. A dreamy little smile spread across my lips, remembering the way Carrie and I would play for hours. Absentmindedly, I lifted my foot over the pattern. When I stomped down on the last square, I looked down at my calf and noticed that it strongly resembled the large, hunking meat of a turkey leg one imagines a medieval king to be gnawing on.

When had this happened? No one ever bought groceries, and I rarely had enough money to eat out, so how had my body expanded so greatly? My brief moment of happiness faded with the realization that if I wanted to be like Carrie, I had a lot to work on. I took a water bottle out of my backpack and chugged half the bottle. Water, I decided, should be my only source of beverage for a while.

I used to be a very big soda drinker. Anything sugary and carbonated was a favorite of mine. On Friday nights, we'd always order a family-sized pizza which would come with two liters of soda, and I'd drink about three glasses and be unable to go to sleep until midnight. If I close my eyes, I can almost smell the sweet, tangy scent of tomato sauce mingling with bubbling cheese and succulent mushrooms. When the pizza arrived, everyone's miserable week would dissipate, and we'd all turn to the television and chow down hungrily as a unit. What I'd give to have that unit again.

I turned into my doorway and saw that the mailbox was bulging again. I raced up the stairs and took out the large bundle of envelopes. As I flipped through them, I saw bill after bill. I know Mom wouldn't remember to pay them, but Dad was back at work. Why wouldn't he be able to do that?

At the bottom of the pile lay a pink envelope. My father's name was scrawled in delicate, floral handwriting. There was no return address, and the stamp featured two personified hearts ogling each other. It seemed a little personal, and after watching way too many *Lifetime* movies, I felt a bit suspicious. I hesitantly brought the letter up to my nose and glanced around to make sure no one was looking at me before I sniffed it. Just as I'd suspected, the undertones of freesia and melon wafted out at me. I wrinkled my nose at the scent, praying that my dad wasn't involved in one of those cliché affairs that take place after a family tragedy. *No way,* I decided. My dad and mom had been in love with each other since the first moment they laid eyes on one another.

My mind, as it was used to doing lately, immediately went back two summers. It had been a beautiful July day, warm and sunny, the scent of freshly cut grass, wildflowers, and lemons filling the air. The family had decided to go to a forest preserve near our house with our German Shepherd, Grizzly. A large, masculine dog, he felt it his duty to bark at everyone and everything, even a bag blowing in the wind, which got really annoying when I'd try to sleep in Saturday mornings.

Our yard was large, but we loved seeing Grizzly run in open spaces, his powerful legs propelling him to unthinkable speeds, the gleam in his eye excited beyond belief when we'd throw a tennis ball.

My mother had packed us a picnic lunch. As a gardener, she was big on presentation, so she'd thrown it in an actual picnic basket adorned with some simple lilies and covered with a checkered blanket. Carrie and I had rolled our eyes at the whole "Yogi-Bear" exhibition, but both secretly loved it. The basket was filled with sandwiches made with turkey, provolone cheese, lettuce, tomato, cucumbers, spinach, and my mother's homemade vinaigrette. There were sliced apples, grapes, sliced cantaloupe, strawberries, and blueberries, along with her homemade chips, which were baked cheddar-infused potatoes. An assortment of water and juices and her famous chocolate mousse torte completed the meal. It was no surprise that we all wanted to eat immediately upon arrival to the preserve, managing to not eat in the car only because my mother guarded the picnic basket as though she were a secret service agent.

As soon as we pulled the car into the parking lot, Grizzly, who'd spent half the trip slobbering on the windows and stumbling around the backseat because he was so large, raced out of the car and furiously began sniffing the trail. We all eagerly bounded behind him, anxious to set up our area and dig into the food. After gorging ourselves senseless, we all reclined on the large, fleece blanket, content to let the sunshine spill onto our faces and listen to the bubbling creek, the rustling of bushes, and the heavy panting of Grizzly, who'd worn himself out and flopped down to join us.

"You know," my dad's voice rumbled, in the midst of our leisure, "this exact moment reminds me of the day that I realized I was in love with your mother."

"Oh, Adrian," my mother laughed, pretending to be bored by the story but clearly delighted.

"Yes," he continued, reaching out to squeeze my mother's hand, stroking a lock of fallen hair away from her eyes. "It all started about fifty years ago," he began playfully, laughing as my mother socked him in the ribs.

"We were on one of our first dates, and man, was I head over heels for this girl! I remember picking her up in my father's Cadillac, a privilege that I got only after forking over gas money, spending the entire day doing odd jobs around the house, and begging him for hours straight. I'd nervously walked to her door, clearing my throat repeatedly and pushing up my sleeves, not knowing what to say. She'd come out with a huge smile on her face, her long hair falling in waves down her back, wearing a little pink dress and white sandals."

"Ad, the dress was not pink!" my mother cried, jabbing him in the side again.

"Hey, give me a break; I'm a guy," he said. "Now, if you'll stop interrupting, I'd like to continue my story." My mother gave him a look, but made no further comments.

"I stared into her blue, blue eyes and asked if she was ready to go, because that's all I could think of to say. She got in the car, and we drove to a little forest a few miles away. We got out and began walking the trail. I remember trying to impress your mother with my Boy

Scout's knowledge, pointing out and naming various trees and plants."

"And I remember pretending to be fascinated but secretly wishing you'd shut up about the difference between Firs and Elms," my mother blurted.

It was my father's turn to give the dirty look, and he tickled her arm before continuing. Andrew had his eyes closed, but I knew he was listening to every word. Carrie had flipped herself onto her stomach, a dreamy look in her eyes as she listened, fascinated. I remained on my back, but treasured the intimate moment, wanting to hear what, precisely, had made my father realize he was in love.

"Anyway," he continued, stretching the word out exaggeratedly, "we'd walked so far and for so long that we'd come to a clearing I was unfamiliar with. To me, it was something that could have only happened in a movie. The space was in a perfect circle, complete with pebbles, a dusting of flowers, and a lone, wooden bench overlooking the lake. It was surrounded by large trees, so even though we could see out into the forest, no one could see us, unless they'd happened to stumble upon the area on accident, as we did.

My heart was pounding wildly, and I couldn't find the words to say. I wanted to kiss your mother badly, but she intimidated me to no end. She smiled at me and waved me over to the bench, her freckles highlighted in the sun. Her slim arms had taken on a slightly reddish tint from walking in the sun. I stopped, reminded myself that I was a man, and began striding over in confidence. Unfortunately, I focused too much on the walking and didn't see the log in front of me.

I flew forward, hit my head on the bench, and fell backwards, clutching my head in embarrassment. Your mother didn't even laugh at me. Instead, she got up, knelt to the ground, took my head in her hands and looked into my eyes, smiling. Then she leaned down, brushed my cheek, and kissed me. This beautiful, intelligent woman liked me, even after I had made a complete fool of myself. I knew then that I would marry her someday. I just had to make her mine."

As my father finished his story, Carrie stared at my parents in adoration, no doubt dreaming up a similar scenario that'd happen to her one day. Andrew remained in his stoic position, but I could sense a slight smile creeping on his lips. My mother had tears in the corners of her eyes but could not stop smiling, and as my father leaned over to plant a kiss on her cheek, I could tell from their warm gazes that they had just as much love for each other now as they had back then. For the rest of the trip, they'd held hands as we walked along the trail, and my father kept his hand on my mother's knee the entire car ride home. I'd thought about their relationship for the rest of the day, wondering what it felt like to be with someone for so long, to have children with them, and to still love each other after so many years, to not be bored with one another.

Definitely not, I decided firmly, tossing the letter for my dad on the table with the rest of the mail. As I sat down and leafed through a gardening magazine that had come in, the pink envelope kept catching my eye. I was so curious, I could barely stand it. I looked to the letter opener, knowing that there was no way I could open it without him knowing. I thought back to all of the crazy television shows and books I've read, wondering what I could do.

Maybe I could steam it open! When I started rummaging for a pot to boil water in, I realized just how psychotic my plan was, and I shook my head, remembering that I wasn't Harriet the Spy or Sherlock Holmes, and that my dad's mail was private. However, just to avoid temptation, I took the letter, raced up to my dad's study, and shoved it under the door. He kept his door locked, so there was no way I could get it now. Immediately afterwards, I felt an odd sensation and flattened myself against the door, wondering precisely why the letter made me feel so weird. I began entertaining multiple ideas in my mind, thinking things like, *Maybe it's from Grandma. Yeah, she likes silly stamps and girly colors. The envelope did have a slight "old-lady" scent going on. Maybe it was for a different Adrian! Maybe one of his clients was just writing to thank him…*

Chapter 10

Finally deciding I had to give it a rest, I walked down to my room, where I put on the first album by *The Strokes*, my favorite band. Carrie had pretended to hate their music, scoffing at their grungy, underground appearance and mocking the lyrics. However, I knew she secretly enjoyed them, because I often caught her humming along or mouthing the lyrics when I played them.

They reminded me of the days we'd be forced to clean our room. Both of us had a bad habit of leaving everything on the floor. When we'd come home from school, we'd toss our clothes on the floor and put on sweatpants, which would be tossed on the floor the next morning. Books, CDs, DVDs, jewelry, perfume, makeup, and shoes littered the floor. Often, there was virtually no path from our floor to the door, and I've stepped on and broken possessions of mine more than once.

When our mother could no longer take it, she'd threaten us with a punishment if we didn't clean our room. Thus, we'd spend full Saturdays doing at least eight loads of laundry, dusting, vacuuming, washing, and spraying our room down. It'd be an all-day project, as we often got distracted by finding old notes or books and stopping to read them. Sometimes, we'd start singing or dancing, and other times, we'd bicker about space. However, we always agreed that we'd clean to music, and we each got an hour's worth of our favorite artist. I'd usually play the Strokes or music from the 80s, which Carrie pretended she loathed, but I know she didn't. She had a softer style, playing folk or indie music, which I thought made me want to sleep, not get stuff done, but she'd wave my comments off in annoyance, softly singing as she folded.

In recent days, my room wasn't as messy because I tended to not care about the things that used to mean so much to me. As I listened to the music, my mind drifted back to the locker room. I decided to lie on my floor and try to do some sit-ups, certain that they would at least do something to control that breakfast sandwich I'd eaten this morning. After managing a few that were extremely uncomfortable with jeans on, I decided to change into some workout-appropriate clothing.

I jogged to the closet (extra points for my new healthy lifestyle) and sifted through the clothes. The left side of the closet (well, the left side and half of the right side) was Carrie's. While most families go through the trouble of removing a loved one's possessions after a death, we didn't do much of that. My parents figured that I would use Carrie's things, and for the most part, I did. On the one hand, it was beneficial to have her items here, because sometimes, they'd provoke great memories within me. Other times, it was just extremely painful, and I'd find myself picking up something as simple as a hairbrush and throwing it against the wall as I'd break down in sobs.

Today though, after my decision to become more like Carrie, I was grateful that my parents hadn't given away her clothes. If there was one thing Carrie had a lot of, it was exercise clothes. I waded through shoes, jeans, corduroy, flannel, silk, and more until I found a neat row of sweatpants, track pants, leggings, sweatshirts, tee-shirts, windbreakers, leg warmers, and gym shoes. I carefully selected a pair of teal leggings, a black V-necked shirt, and a purple sweatband.

Honestly, I didn't need the sweatband, nor did I find it particularly aiding during my exercise, but I thought it'd help me feel the part of someone who was dedicated to fitness. Once I'd changed and brushed my tangled, soup-soaked locks into a ponytail, I was ready to start again. I lay flat on my back, pulled my knees together, and lifted my upper body, intent on mimicking the way Carrie would do crunches and sit-ups every night before bed.

I can remember her doing what seemed like hundreds of sit-ups, her breathing loud but her glances in the mirror admirable. I'd yawn exaggeratedly and repeatedly ask her to be quiet so I could get to sleep, but she'd always sneer in my direction and ignore me. After managing to do about 25 without stopping, I felt proud of myself. That was 25 more than I'd done in, well, ever. For the first time that day, a smile came over my face. Then I made the mistake of looking to the mirror as I tried another sit-up. As my body contorted forward, a wide ribbon of flab was squeezed between my chest and hips. I panicked before I reached down, terrified that I could grab a large chunk of my stomach in one hand, feeling no muscles, just a pure, doughy-like material.

As earlier, I questioned when this had happened. Although I didn't find myself to be supermodel material, I'd always been comfortable with myself. I'd never dream of imagining I was fat, as I'd always loathed skinny girls who would whine in nasally voices about how fat they were and how they simply must lose weight. Give me a break. Yet here I was, suddenly examining every inch of my body and hating it in ways I'd never even considered before.

My fingers, which were always praised for being long and thin, (piano fingers, my mother liked to call them) looked like plump little encased sausages. My wrists seemed larger than ever, almost the same width as my forearm. Even my face felt chubby, and my hands were able to grab a couple inches of skin from my cheeks.

I sighed and felt miserable at that moment, knowing that no one would respect me in the likeness of Carrie since I was just a pig in a sweatband, an animal that shouldn't even be allowed near her goddess-like self. I walked closer to the mirror and glared at myself. *No more,* I decided. Needing inspiration and someone to talk to, I dove onto my bed and slid halfway off of it backwards, reaching beneath it to extract the diary from the box. Opening the book from where I'd left off, I was eager to read the next day's entry.

Today was better than yesterday only because I'd started my plan and stuck to it. This morning, at breakfast, I told Mom that I didn't feel very well and couldn't stomach the pancakes. This was met with glee by Felicia and Andrew, who gobbled mine down as if there was no tomorrow. Disgusting! Felicia is lucky she has a good metabolism, or she'd turn out chubby like me. As usual, Mom handed each of us bags of lunch, and without even glancing inside, I knew there was some kind of sweet treat in there. When we got to school, I casually tossed it in the trash can without letting Felicia see. At lunch, my friends asked me where my food was, but I pretended I felt sick again and told them I'd eat some soup when I got home. By dinnertime, I was feeling a little dizzy, so I pushed around the food on my plate, eating only two carrots and some turnips. My mother looked at me worriedly throughout the meal, but I assured her it was probably one of those bugs and retreated to the bedroom. There, I drank two glasses of water, did 50 sit-ups, 50 crunches, 50 push-ups, and lifted three math books 25 times on each arm. When I finally crawled into bed, I was tired, but there is no greater feeling than realizing you made it through the day without giving in to temptation.

After reading, I felt mixed emotions. First, I was a little appalled that she thought it was disgusting that Andrew and I were eating pancakes. That seemed a bit extreme. Then, I was worried that she'd been sneaking around and no one had noticed. I tried to remember the day she was talking about, but I really couldn't. Still, if she could do it, so could I. Plus, I had the advantage of having no food in the house to begin with and no parents to monitor my choices. I quietly closed the diary and tucked it back under the bed, laying on my bed and staring at the ceiling. I fell asleep with the lights on, but before I drifted off to sleep, I had visions of long, lean limbs dancing in my head.

Chapter 11

The next morning, I headed down to the kitchen and saw something that made me stop in my tracks: my mother. Since Carrie died, she was rarely seen out of her bedroom, and when she was, it was usually to go to the bathroom. She was dressed in an old, baggy sweatshirt and a pair of jeans. The jeans, dark-rinse denim that usually looked great on her, sagged around the waist and knees, bunching up in places. Her hair, which was usually trimmed every six weeks, now fell down her back in scraggly locks, uneven and split. When she heard my cautious footsteps, she turned around, her usually bright eyes looking rather pale, ornamented by deep, purple bags.

"Hi, Felicia," she managed weakly, her voice rough and scratchy. She stood in front of the coffee-pot, staring as though she couldn't figure out precisely how it worked anymore.

"Um, hi," I said. Since when did things start getting so awkward around my parents? I didn't like it at all. "Need help there, Mom?" I asked, gesturing towards the coffee.

"Oh, no," she said, reaching for a glass and filling it with water.

"Are you alright?" I asked hesitantly, the creases of my eyes wrinkling in concern. Before she could answer, my father entered the back door, wearing a rumpled suit. All in the kitchen at the same time, something that hardly ever happened in the last ten months, we stared awkwardly at one another, unsure of who should speak first.

"Penny," my father started in surprise, probably in as much disbelief as I was that she was in the kitchen. My mother jerked her head up sharply, almost as if she'd already forgotten he was in the room.

41

"Good morning," she mumbled in reply, tugging her shirt down, her shoulders visibly shrinking.

"When I left the bedroom you were still sleeping," my father said almost nervously, twisting the cuffs of his pressed pale blue shirt.

"Oh, when you left at 1:00 in the morning?" my mother snapped, her eyes narrowing and her cheeks turning red, one of the first instances I'd seen color on her face in months. My father took a step back, shocked at her tone and the challenge she flung at him, puzzled by the rising altercation, something that hadn't taken place in quite a while for them.

He raised his eyebrows and popped the latches on his briefcase a few times before stammering, "I didn't leave the house, Penny. I just went downstairs to watch some television because I couldn't sleep and I didn't want to wake you."

His eyes avoided hers, and she stared at him a moment before retreating back to her safe place, the glass of water she'd poured untouched. My father didn't acknowledge me, instead grabbing his briefcase and hurrying out the front door, shutting it quickly but quietly. I stood alone in the kitchen, wondering how to absorb what had just occurred. My mind wandered back to the letter that had been placed under my father's door. Had he opened it? Was some woman out there, desperately awaiting his response?

I closed my eyes and felt my hands slowly clenching into fists, breathing deeply for a moment before wracking my brain for common stress relievers. People liked to smoke when they were stressed, but I'm pretty sure I couldn't get access to cigarettes. I couldn't afford a trip to the spa, and I didn't want to relax. The light bulb went on when I pictured myself running around the neighborhood. Sure, I'd never really run purposely before, but how hard could it be? It's just a faster version of walking. A smile spread over my face as I realized that running would burn some extra calories and probably move me closer to my goal of being like Carrie. At that point, I decided that I would begin running every morning and try to do it during evenings as well.

I raced upstairs and grabbed a pair of basketball shorts, a white tee-shirt and some old Nikes of Carrie's. I shook my hair into a ponytail and grabbed a bottle of water before heading out the door.

Remembering that Carrie used to stretch out on the living room floor before she'd go running, I bent over and attempted to touch my toes a few times, but that didn't go over too well.

The first time I leaned down, I couldn't quite reach my toes, and the second time I tried, I tipped right over into the grass, my face meeting a pile of dirt. Shaking myself off, I got up and began running, instantly feeling better the second my foot hit the pavement. The sun was beating down, spreading a blanket of warmth over my face. My hair tumbled down my back, my ponytail flying up and down as I made my strides. Before long, I was breathing hard and needed to stop. While running, I hadn't really been paying attention to where I was, instead focusing on the feeling of being outside. When I finally looked up, I realized I had barely gone a block before I'd felt winded. My sides ached and my chest felt tight.

An extreme feeling of disappointment washed over me, in disbelief that I was so out of shape that I could barely run for a block before getting tired. I pinched the loose flesh of my stomach, disgusted that there was skin to grab onto. As I'd been running, I'd noticed that my legs jiggled and possessed various crevices I'd never paid attention to before. I'd always thought my legs were muscular from the bike riding and walking I did, but this new revelation that my legs were chubby spun my world.

I'd never had a problem with my body before, knowing that I wasn't fat and that for the most part, I ate well and exercised enough. My mind strained to remember Carrie's body the last time I'd seen her. Her shoulder bones jutted out and her knees were knobby, but she'd looked good. It was funny. At the time, I remember everyone being so worried about her, claiming that she needed to eat better and gain some weight. I'd agreed with them, staring at her bony limbs in a mixture of concern and disgust. Now though, I remember that image as one that was beautiful.

Her appearance had been striking. She was of average height, but the weight she'd lost had instantly made her seem taller, in possession of a body a model would have. Her face had once been adorable, her cheeks slightly fuller, so that anyone who looked at her would think of a cherub. Later, her face became sharp and angular, making her look older. Her hollowed cheekbones lent mystery to her face, her appearance one of secrets and loss; it was a face that no one could decode. Her legs, once muscular and shapely, looked as though they had been whittled down, carved into two long, lean, sticks, bony and bruised up close, but miles high in a short dress.

A dreamy look crossed my face as I pictured myself achieving that same body, walking into school wearing all black, oblivious to the admiring stares, my face the epitome of cool. My dream is cut short when I trip over a crack in the sidewalk. My arms flailed wildly in the air and my chin skidded across the grass, a lovely green streak wrapping itself around the side of my neck. I groaned in annoyance, a sharp pain shooting through my leg.

Chapter 12

"Need some help?" a quiet, deep voice asked. My face burned in embarrassment, and I looked up into the eyes of Julian, warm and hazel today. I opened my mouth to speak, but nothing came out. Every time he'd seen me this week, I'd been in some sort of distress. Just like before, he was only available to play the part of the hero. I was suddenly filled with anger, both that every time he caught me I was doing something stupid and that he always seemed to show up when it was convenient for him to do some saving.

"No!" I finally snapped, pushing myself up with my hands. I then noticed the trickle of blood falling down my knee, the wound dark and filled with small bits of gravel. The sight turned my stomach, but I tried to remain poised and in control. Before he could say another word, I turned on my heel and ran. I was about a half a block away before the pain kicked in, and at that point, I could only limp.

I knew it was a mistake, but I had to see him again. I turned around and caught him sitting on the curb, his head in his hands. His entire body looked as though it could crumple at any second. A shiver of remorse ran through me, realizing that in much the same way I had, he'd lost his best friend. And it was my fault. My eyes filled with tears and I swiped at them furiously, angry at myself for showing emotion. I did what I do best and banished the feeling away deep inside of me, opening my mind to thoughts of my new diet plan and limped my way home.

When I reached the house, it was quiet as always, the strange occurrence that had taken place earlier no longer overpowering the kitchen. The glass of water that my mother had poured still stood on the counter, so I tossed an ice cube in there and gulped it down. Due to my unwillingness to wake up extra early, I didn't have too long to get ready.

My "Carrie" routine wouldn't go into full effect today, but I'd do my best. After quickly showering, I brushed some shadow at the corner of my lids, flicked a mascara wand through my lashes and put a feather clip into my hair. As I fastened it, thoughts of Julian came to mind. He had been the first person I'd given one of my feather creations to, and when I'd handed him the necklace, his face had lit up and he'd given me a huge hug. I haven't done any crafts since Carrie.

I shook my head and walked to Carrie's side of the closet. My style had been called many things, but hip and fashion-forward usually wasn't one of them. My clothes included a variety of patterns, especially floral. I had plenty of V-necked tee shirts, and lots of pencil-leg trousers, skinny jeans, and cigarette pants. I favored dresses and cardigans, had a drawer full of colorful tights, and tended to wear clothes reminiscent of the 80s, things one would find in a thrift store.

Carrie would often wrinkle her nose when I'd bring home a new piece of clothing, unable to see the treasure that I'd see in it. My shoe collection contained oxfords, moccasins, combat boots, and ballet flats in almost every color of the rainbow. My wardrobe was a far cry from the designer jeans, pastel sweaters, heels, and skirts Carrie's contained. However, I know that she admired the way I chose to wear clothes that other peers didn't approve of. When her friends whispered mindlessly about my choice of fishnets with shorts, I could see Carrie's lips struggling not to curl into a smile, proud that I hadn't hopped on the bandwagon and fallen down the popularity hole.

Today, however, I gravitated towards her side and ran my hands over her dresses. As I rustled through them, the scent of freesia and melon wafted through the air, causing my eyes to immediately sting with tears. I hadn't smelled that perfume in months, and it instantly brought me back to vivid memories of Carrie. I clung to the dress, holding it close to my chest before I collapsed into a heap on the floor, silently sobbing at the bottom of my closet.

By the time I'd managed to get out of the closet, I had already missed first period. I'd cried all my makeup off and my hair, still wet, had molded itself into a weird wave on the side of my head. Rather than take another shower and make it in time for third period, I decided to just stay home. Neither of my parents would notice, and I knew I wouldn't miss anything at school. I already had multiple overdue assignments; what were a few more? Now I could spend the day burning calories.

I walked to the garage and located my bike, a difficult task since it was buried under a mountain of other bikes. At a time, my family was extremely athletic. We used to strap our bikes to the top of our car and drive up to a variety of trails and forest preserves, biking over sand, gravel, concrete, and grass for miles upon miles, a sweet escape from the loud, hectic city. After lifting the other bikes off of mine and scratching and bruising my legs in every possible place in the process, I took a paper towel and wiped off some of the cobwebs that were arranged haphazardly over the seat and through the spokes. I didn't know how far I was going to ride, but I knew that I had to get away from here.

I wasn't sure if five minutes or two hours had passed, but I'd come to a secluded, wooded area. I inhaled the fresh scent of pine, let the sun beat down on my face, and felt the familiar crunching of leaves and gravel below my feet. There was nowhere I felt better than in the forest. There was something incredibly soothing about being amongst nature, and I felt as though my deepest and most profound thinking was done there. If only my American Literature teacher could see me now, behaving as though I was Henry Thoreau.

I chained my bike near the entrance and began hiking deep into the woods, trying my hardest to absorb the beauty I was passing but generally only seeing the tree as brownish-green blurs. At one point, my legs felt as though they were going to give out, so I sat on a log. It was an unusually small log, almost abnormally thin and a rich brown that didn't quite mirror the brown of the other trees. I almost smiled to myself, finding it fitting that I would sit there. I leaned back and closed my eyes, allowing visions of the future to take over me.

Thinking about my parent's first date, I tried to imagine myself with someone in the forest. I pictured myself in cutoff jean shorts and a flowered tank top, my hair in a messy bun and a carefree smile on my face. Of course, I'd be about twenty pounds lighter. In my fantasy, my shoulder bones and clavicles protruded in an attractive way, and my legs were thin and toned without an ounce of fat on them. I continued the daydream, imagining myself walking along, a pair of muscled arms encased in a flannel shirt suddenly wrapping themselves around my waist. I squealed and turned around, only to look up into the smiling face of...Julian?

I felt flustered for a moment, embarrassed even though no one could see me. I'm not one of those girls in books and movies that pretend like she isn't in love with her best friend and is suddenly shocked when she can't stop thinking about him. I do have special feelings for Julian, and I've always been attracted to him. He's the most beautiful boy I have ever seen. But there is absolutely no way that I could ever have a romantic relationship with him. The things I've said to him can't be taken back. And he's such a good guy. His constant worrying about me will get in the way of my main goal, and if I want to look like Carrie, I can't have anyone worrying about me.

Chapter 13

The rest of the month passed by somewhat uneventfully. It's amazing how slowly and quickly time can go by after someone dies. There are days that feel like eternities and days that feel like seconds. This month had gone by in an instant, yet it seemed like my diet had done nothing for my body. I had almost no recollection of the events, excluding my run-in with Julian. When I turned the key in the lock, the house was dark and silent, which wasn't unusual. However, when I flipped the light on, I heard muffled sobbing. On instinct, I immediately ran upstairs to my parent's bedroom, but when I tried to turn the knob, I found that it was locked.

"Mom?" I called tentatively, not really expecting an answer. My suspicion was confirmed a few moments later, as the sobbing stopped and I was met with complete silence again. I sighed and rubbed my eyes, wondering if my mother was crying about Carrie or if something serious was going on between her and my father. Again, I wasn't about to go all Nancy Drew, but their confrontation this morning had left me unsettled. Although my father often worked on cases during odd hours, I wasn't sure I could ever remember him actually leaving the house. I decided I'd look into it more tomorrow and headed to my room.

As I surveyed the expanse of my familiar, teal room, I felt an odd pang in my stomach. At that moment, there was nothing I wanted more than to be thin, happy, and like Carrie. I stared at my collection of vinyl, CDs and cassettes, items that had once been my favorite in the room and suddenly felt like they were just an obstacle to my goal. My heart beating furiously, I lunged forward, gathered them up into

49

my arms and flung them onto the floor. The bookshelf that housed a number of classics, fiction, and even silly romance novels was ransacked, each book carelessly thrown into the closet, even though in the past, I'd be angry if anyone even bent one of my pages. Some satchels, purses, and large bags hung on the side of my bed, and they were far too edgy and "thrift-store-esque" to fit in with Carrie's crowd.

I grabbed them all and flipped them over, dumping out vintage compacts, mermaid, pearl, and shell hair combs, and strings of pearls, all of which seemed to fall in slow motion to the floor. As I destroyed my room, I could feel that I was destroying a piece of myself, a burning sensation that started in my throat and settled somewhere in my heart. There was a longing that rested in my chest, telling me that it was Carrie's stuff I should be getting rid of, now my own. I shoved that thought aside just as I'd shoved my belongings everywhere.

When I was satisfied with the way my room looked, I decided that it was time to exercise. I'd done quite well for the day. I'd been so distracted with thoughts of my parents, ditching school, and trying to reorganize my room that food had been the furthest thing from my mind. I came up with a brief routine that consisted of 50 sit-ups, 50 squats, and then 50 push-ups, and would repeat it for as many times as I could. When I finished, I walked over to the mirror. I don't know what I'd expected to see, but my disappointment was extreme.

I knew that my body wouldn't transform in just a few days, but I thought that maybe my legs would look at least a little tighter, or my stomach would suck in a little further. I looked the same as I'd looked the day in the locker room, if not heavier. My legs looked chunky and rippled, and my arms seemed to look thick and solid, a far cry from the willowy, pipe-cleaner arms I so desperately yearned for and envisioned in my head.

Tears crept into the corner of my eyes, threatening to spill over at any minute. No matter how hard I worked, I knew I could never be like Carrie. Not unless I just refused to eat. The idea was a stupid one, yes, but just imagining having enough control to go for days without eating brought a smile to my face. I knew that I wasn't ugly, but I'd never been asked on a date before. Carrie got asked on dates all the time. Once I got a bit thinner, perhaps I'd find myself doing more than sitting in front of the television on a Friday night, shoveling potato chips and ice cream into my mouth.

For the first night in a while, I crawled into bed with a content feeling. I didn't reach under the bed to pull out Carrie's diary, feeling in my heart that I was one step closer to becoming someone she'd have wanted to be friends with. Yes, we were sisters, twins, even, but when high school rolled around, our connection seemed lost somehow. We didn't talk as much as we used to and she was always intent on being with other people, people who weren't me. As I held my pillow closed to my chest, I wished she could see me now, my hair long and shining (I once got a pixie cut that she nearly fainted at the sight of), wearing clothes that she'd approve of, and building a body that she'd be envious of. Of course I wasn't near the last part, but I would be.

My own word choice struck me in an unusual way. Why had I chosen to say build? My family was pretty religious, and I had faith in God. Shouldn't I leave the 'building of my body' to Him? The question lasted in my mind only briefly; for after Carrie died, everyone seemed to lose a bit of their faith. We no longer attended church regularly, and even though Andrew attended a religious university, our former religious traditions seemed to have fallen somewhere down the line and were in no sight of being retrieved any time soon. My eyes soon closed, and I slept dreamlessly.

Chapter 14

When I woke the next morning, I knew things were different. I felt renewed, filled with a vigor I hadn't felt in quite a while. I stretched and delicately slid my feet to the floor, pretending my legs were long and lithe, weightless as they slung over the side of my bed. I hummed to myself as I took a swig from the water bottle on the side of my bed and struck a pose in front of the mirror.

I had some serious bed-head, but there was something daring about its rumpled, messy quality. I pouted and leaned forward, running my fingers over my clavicles and thinking about how far they'd jut out in the future. There must have been something rewarding about each day of Carrie's process. I knew that once I started seeing results, things would begin shaping up. I'd have friends besides Jack Kerouac and Kurt Vonnegut.

Grizzly pushed his way into my room and trotted over to me, his mouth stretched into what looked like a smile, his pants obvious laughter at my ridiculousness. I narrowed my eyes at him, but he was so adorable I couldn't be mad at him. I felt bad for him, in fact. Ever since Carrie died, he almost never got taken for walks or played with anymore. I gave him a few pats in a lame attempt to make up for it.

In between pursing my lips and raising my eyebrows, I caught a faint conversation that sounded as though it was coming from down the hall. I stopped where I was, letting my feet sink into the plush carpet. I could make out hushed voices, but I couldn't determine actual words. I dropped to my stomach and did a sort of army crawl towards my door, opening it slightly.

"I've asked you at least a million times to page me, not call me on my office phone!" My dad's voice was urgent and insistent, spitting out words in suppressed tones. There was silence for a moment, and then I heard his voice again, this time soothing and relaxed.

"I know, I know. And that means the world to me. I just can't risk it right now, you must understand that. I will, and I'm looking forward to it." A low chuckle sounded before his voice became so low I could no longer hear his whispers.

My whole body started to shake and my stomach felt as though it were a bowling bowl being hurtled toward pins. I'm pretty sure that I broke out in an actual sweat. Although my mind was racing with what seemed like thousands of thoughts, I shut all of them off and ran downstairs. I threw open the refrigerator, gagging at the odor of mustard and sweet and sour sauce that it emitted. I cursed myself for forgetting that the refrigerator held nothing and slammed it shut, immediately opening the freezer.

I could choose between frozen spaghetti and meat balls, frozen lasagna, or frozen rice casserole. Deciding not to choose, I dumped them all onto a large plate and stuck it in the microwave. While I waited, I felt ravenous, so I opened the pantry and poured some stale cereal into a bowl. We didn't have milk, but I was so hungry that I splashed water on top of it and shoveled spoonful after spoonful into my mouth, barely tasting the cardboard-like flakes. When the timer on the microwave dinged, I took the plate out and forked it into my mouth as fast as I could, not minding if the spaghetti sauce got on the rice mixture. Even though it was tasteless to me, it was extremely comforting.

When I finally finished, I felt as though my stomach were carrying twins, possibly even triplets. I'd never felt as heavy and full before, and I was so disgusted with myself that I burst into tears. I didn't want to think about my father, and I didn't want to think about what I had just done. I decided that I needed Carrie more than ever at this moment, and I talked to her as I went upstairs in search of her journal, begging her to send me some kind of sign. Should I pursuit the strangeness orbiting around my father? Was it something serious, or did I just have an overactive imagination and a penchant for spy movies?

When I reached my room, I fell onto my bed backwards and reached underneath it, removing the journal from the box in one swift motion. I opened it up to the page I left off on, prepared to read some sort of glamorous highlight from her life. Instead, I was greeted with something very different.

I've been doing so well lately. For the entire week, I've managed to eat only fruits, vegetables, and some fat-free yogurt. Whenever my energy levels get low, I just pop some sliced strawberries into my mouth and slowly begin to feel better. I haven't noticed any incredible changes yet, but the band on my workout pants feels a bit looser. I was afraid that I'd ruined everything today, though. When I got home from school, I was hungrier than I'd felt in a long time. Felicia and Andrew were out, and Mom and Dad were still at work. There is nothing I love more than having the house to myself, and when I do, I usually cook or bake something special for me. The craving to eat when I got home hit me hard. I did everything I could, from trying to distract myself with homework to literally leaving the house. These attempts were futile, though, and eventually, I found myself standing in front of the open refrigerator in awe, staring at the mountain of food it contained. Before I knew it, I'd made myself a humongous sandwich, gobbled half a FAMILY size bag of potato chips, ate two brownies, and gulped two large glasses of soda. The sad part is, I was still hungry. I melted cheese onto three tortillas with avocado on top, convincing myself that it was good since I was including produce. Then I had a bowl of ice cream and three granola bars. This was more food than I'd consumed the entire week, and when I had finished my binge, even though my stomach was impossibly full, I felt empty inside. I'd given up a week of hard work to stuff myself senseless, and the pleasure was extremely short-lived. In a panic, I decided to try something I'd read about in magazines. Even though I was extremely ashamed, I felt as though I had nowhere else to turn. I locked the bathroom door, blasted the radio, and stuck my finger down my throat. At first, nothing happened. I coughed and felt tears well up in my eyes, but no food came out. In a fit of anger, I jammed my finger further down my mouth, feeling it scrape against the side of my throat. Finally, I felt sweat break out and saw half of my binge in the toilet. I felt as though I needed to get rid of every ounce of food I'd inhaled, so I repeated the process at least three times. Afterward, my throat felt raw and my face was hot and tear-stained, but nothing could stop the smile from spreading across my face. I'd found a way to have my cake and eat it too.

My hand covered my mouth, completely in shock at what I'd just read. Carrie and I had sat in out room together and watched a cheesy Lifetime movie featuring a bulimic girl, and we both swore up and down that we'd never resort to something like that. We'd laughed about it! It broke my heart to know that we'd drifted so far that we could keep such serious things from each other.

How did I have no idea that this was going on? A tear rolled down my cheek, but a thought struck me that caused the waterfall threatening to burst from behind my eyelids to cease. Although it was probably a bit of a stretch, I thought there was some sort of connection occurring here. Who knew that the day I'd have my own wild binge would be the day I'd read about Carrie's? And who knew that she was such a striking writer? She'd always been good at English, but her diary entries read almost like narratives. They managed to reach me in a way that was chillingly persuasive.

Never in my life had I even considered doing something that I found repulsive and weak. Yet in my desperateness to be close to my dead sister, my need to rid my stomach of the food I'd just gorged myself on, and a way to keep the weight-loss journey going, I somehow found myself hovering over the toilet, frozen.

It was almost as though I'd left my body. My ears hurt from the silence, and my eyes seemed to be opening and closing without my permission. I knew this was something I didn't want to get myself into, but the need to make my stomach feel empty again was almost too strong for me to fight against. I slumped to the floor and gripped the side of the sink, saying a silent prayer to Carrie and begging her to guide me, begging her journal to reveal that she'd never repeated such a disgusting act again. I chided myself one last time, trying to force myself to remember how utterly vile throwing up was. But it was no use. My mind had made the decision.

Unlike Carrie, I was successful in my first attempt. As the food spilled out of me, my throat burned, but I felt an immense relief, my stomach lighter and my mind clearer. Most of all, I'd felt something I hadn't felt in a long time: control. The power that surged through my veins was almost too much to handle. Yes, I was a disgusting pig who ate far more than she should have, but I had taken care of it and no longer had to worry about this roadblock.

An eerie calm settled over me as I flushed the toilet and splashed my face with water. I brushed my teeth and slowly brought my head up to the mirror. I didn't just see splotchy red patches on my pale skin, under-eye circles, and sweaty bangs. I saw something I'd never expected to see so soon. I saw Carrie.

Chapter 15

By the time the intensity of the morning was over, it was almost nine. I shuddered to think that I'd eaten frozen dinners for breakfast, but at least I felt a bit better about going to school, even though I'd be late. I decided to ask my father to write me an excuse note, which would also give me a chance to try to scope out the situation.

I burst into his office without knocking, something I knew annoyed him beyond belief. He looked up, startled as I breezed into the room. I walked briskly over to him and planted my hands onto the desk, looking down at him as though I were a scrutinizing detective.

"Yes, Felicia?" he asked, clearly confused and agitated.

"I need an excuse note for school. I woke up late."

He raised his eyebrows and bit down on his lip. I recognized his "lecture face" and almost wanted to start laughing. This man, a man who was possibly having an affair less than a year after my sister died and at a time when my family needed him the most was about to lecture me for sleeping through an alarm clock?

In an effort to change the subject and a typical case of my not thinking before I opened my mouth, I questioned him. "So who were you on the phone with?"

My father's expression changed to one of shock and panic before settling into a serious, hardened expression.

"A client," he said firmly. "But I don't recall you ever expressing much of an interest in my business."

The room suddenly felt chilly, and even though my father was a few feet away from me, it seemed as though I were standing atop a mountain and looking through a pair of binoculars at a tiny ant miles and miles away. He noticed my shocked expression and was quick to put a smile on his face, one that was clearly forced as the lines in his face revealed his tenseness. He reached over his desk for a piece of stationary and quickly jotted down a two-line note, handing it to me in a matter of seconds, as though he were trying to get me out of his office as quickly as possible. I held the paper in my hands for a moment, looking at him in confusion. He'd already picked up a pen and was writing on an important-looking document, his silent source of dismissal.

I backed away slowly in disbelief, pain ringing through my entire body. My throat felt raw and scratchy, but I knew that wasn't the only thing holding me back from all the words I wanted to say. I stood in the doorway a minute longer, but my father never even looked up, even though I knew he knew I was there. I was going to get to the bottom of this. Never mind all of my cartoon spy fantasies. My family had been through too much in the last year to start breaking apart now. There was no way I was going to let him hurt us like this.

After raiding Carrie's side of the closet and fashioning my hair into a quick side braid, I was off to school. I no longer received sympathetic looks when I presented my late notes in the office. Instead, they were looks of suspicion and concern. I had the grace to look guilty and sort of slunk away after my note was stamped with a glare of disapproval. I hurried out of the office and began walking briskly toward my classroom, a feat made slightly more difficult in the pinched black flats I was wearing. Carrie and I may have been identical, but my feet had always been a bit wider than hers. Trying to ignore the blisters that must have been forming at my heels, I noticed the quiet hall wasn't as empty as I thought it was.

I needed to go to my locker, but I saw a tall figure with familiar dark locks reaching into the locker next to mine. I still wasn't ready to face Julian. I strategically shifted my chin to the left so that he wouldn't see my eyes on him. It was then that I realized he wasn't alone. He stood with another girl, who was staring up at him and laughing as though he were the funniest boy in the world. She had short, choppy reddish-blonde hair and wore a floral dress, navy tights, and black boots, an outfit much like one I'd have worn in the past. She hugged her books to her chest before reaching out and placing her hand on his arm, smiling flirtatiously.

My heart started pounding and my stomach felt as though someone had rammed a medicine ball into it. Who was this mystery girl and why had I never seen her before? Julian tended to be a loner. Before Carrie, we'd spent almost all our time together and there weren't many other people in the picture. I can't imagine where he'd met her, how they began talking, or why she felt so comfortable with him that she could touch him so easily. I was instantly jealous, not only of her obvious familiarity with Julian, but with her ability to wear the kind of clothes I had to eliminate from my wardrobe. I immediately chastised myself, realizing there was no reason for me to think possessively. I was the one that threw our friendship away. I had no right to be worried about who he was with.

My stare probably grew too intense. Within seconds, Julian glanced up, his expression a mixture of confusion, concern, and curiosity. I instantly looked away, even though I knew he had already caught me and that I was probably making it more awkward. I started walking as fast as I could, which turned out to be a foolish decision since I slipped on a piece of notebook paper and fell a few feet in front of the two.

"Felicia," Julian called, abandoning Locker Girl to come to my aid.

Refusing to allow him to get near, I got up in a scramble and managed to choke out, "I'm fine." I dusted the front of my sweater and broke out in a run, reaching my classroom in just under twenty seconds. As stupid as it was, I couldn't help but look back. Julian remained at the spot I'd been in a heap in moments before, staring after me in bewilderment. The girl stood awkwardly by the locker, staring at Julian. The whole scene was so ridiculous I almost laughed. But nothing in my life was funny at the moment, and there was no reason to exercise my mouth muscles for anything but talking when necessary.

The hours of the day seemed to stretch on forever. I tried as hard as I could to pay attention in all my classes, but my mind couldn't drift from Julian. We'd run into each other so many times it was almost comical by now, and each time he seemed to want to talk to me, but I was too embarrassed by my behavior. Sometimes I would sit at my desk and my mind would go blank, and then I'd congratulate myself for going at least five seconds without thinking of him or his locker lady. Something didn't settle right when I thought of the two of them together.

By the time I got home, all I wanted to do was go to sleep. When Carrie first passed away, all I would do after school was sleep. It was the only way to escape, and sometimes I wished that I'd never wake up. Today was one of those days.

Chapter 16

When I finally woke, darkness streamed through my windows, the faint light of the moon casting a silvery shadow over my crumpled form. I struggled to sit up, and when I did, everything went black for a moment and my head began pounding. I realized that I hadn't had anything to eat all day and immediately felt better. So my father was possibly cheating on my mother and my best friend had found someone else. At least I was on the way to becoming a prettier, better me. A me that Carrie wouldn't be embarrassed to be seen with.

Since I'd slept from after school into the night, I was awake before my alarm clock went off. I decided to use this opportunity as a chance to go running. It was only 5, so my parents weren't awake yet. After slipping on black yoga pants and a navy sweatshirt, I silently tiptoed down the stairs and filled a bottle with water. I decided to take a path that lead to a small pond hidden behind large, graceful willow trees. It used to be a favorite spot of mine and Carrie's. The last time we'd been there was a time I wished I could forget.

It was a cold Saturday evening. The family had been having dinner. Mom had made an incredible meal of homemade ravioli stuffed with ricotta and spinach, bruschetta, and tomato and mozzarella salad. As usual, Carrie had spent most of dinner pushing her meal around her plate and picking at the salad. Since this had been occurring for the past few weeks, my mother could no longer contain her annoyance.

"Carrie," she had said, "I think you're a little too old to be playing with your food. Stick your fork into a ravioli, stick the ravioli into your mouth, and eat it." Carrie had glared at her but didn't answer, angrily stuffing a leaf of romaine into her mouth. When sufficient time had passed and Carrie still hadn't eaten, my mom exploded.

"I asked you to eat your dinner! You think I haven't noticed how loose your clothes have been fitting lately? Living healthy is one thing, but not eating is another. I refuse to allow you to lose any more weight, and since you're not going to cooperate, I'm going to start monitoring your meals. How do you feel about that?"

Carrie rolled her eyes, but they filled with tears. She pushed her plate to the middle of the table, knocking over a glass of water. Everyone gawked at her in surprise; she was hardly one to engage in such behavior. She almost knocked her chair over as she got up, running out the door in only a tee-shirt and jeans. Before my parents could react, I grabbed a sweater hanging on the stair banister and ran out after her.

"Carrie!" I called, out of breath after only a few minutes. "Carrie, wait!"

"Leave me alone!" she yelled back, an obvious sob in her scream.

The coolness of the night made my lungs feel as if they were going to expand right out of my rib cage. I stopped for a minute, leaning over and grabbing my knees, huffing and puffing as if I were an old lady. It was alright if I stopped. I knew where she was going.

Once I got on the trail, I paused to take in the serenity and beauty of the night, such a contrast to the table scene that had played out minutes before. The leaves almost looked as if they'd been dipped in gold, brilliant against the dark wood. The further I walked, the more visible the stars became, little jewels glistening against a black blanket that stretched across the earth. I wished that I could convince Carrie she was just as beautiful.

As I neared the pond, I saw her silhouette, slight and angular, a shadow so small it could almost be overlooked. It really hit me then how tiny she'd become. Her shoulders now appeared hunched at all times, her collarbone jutting out in a way that was almost unnatural. Her legs, which had already been slender, now appeared lean and delicate, almost as if someone had shaved off inches of skin. Even though she looked so fragile that she could easily be broken, there was still something almost magical about her beauty.

"Carrie," I said softly, unsure of how to approach. She didn't answer me, instead continuing to throw small pebbles into the water. Moonlight bounced off the top of each pebble and created a beam of light, more proof that there was something enchanting about her. I cautiously made my way over to her, stepping over mud and puddles and dodging low-slung branches. I put my hand over her shoulder, and almost backed away in shock when I felt how small it was under her oversized shirt. I could probably fit both of her shoulders in one palm.

She was shivering and sweating, quite the opposite of her usual calm, stoic demeanor. After what seemed like an eternity of silence, she turned and looked at me. Her eyes contained no warmth whatsoever, instead two circles of ice. When she finally spoke, the muscles around her mouth barely moved, almost as if she didn't have the energy or effort to speak to me.

"You shouldn't have followed me here. There is nothing you can do and I have nothing to say to you. Go home, please."

I ignored her cold words and plopped down next to her, a rather large mistake since I sat in a small puddle of water, something that would haunt me on the chilly walk home.

"Carrie, what Mom said is true. You're already super skinny. If you get any skinnier, we won't be able to see you! She cares about you, you know. That's all! Hey, why don't we stop to get ice cream on the way back?" I was rambling on and on, my mind already picturing a waffle cone filled with rich, chocolate ice cream and smothered in hot fudge and peanuts.

"Ice cream?" Carrie shrieked, her voice unnaturally high. "You think I want ice cream? Can you not see the pillows of fat on my body? And you're trying to feed me ice cream?"

My eyes widened with panic. I hadn't heard her freak out this badly since I ripped the head off her favorite doll in 3rd grade. She continued to rant, although I could only make out "idiot" and "are you kidding me?" more than a few times. Her fingers dug into the ground next to her and her jaw moved furiously. She reminded me of a cartoon character, but instead of finding it funny, I was actually quite frightened.

The next thing I knew, Carrie picked up a medium sized rock and flung it directly at my nose. I staggered backward, the pain and shock blinding me for a moment. I landed on a piece of ground that was made up of dirt, mud, water, and wet leaves that smelled delightful. She walked away then, still mumbling and heatedly shredding a fistful of leaves. She reminded me at that moment of a mad scientist, or maybe just mad.

Without bothering to glance behind her, she walked further into the path until she was completely shrouded by the willow trees, leaving me to fend for myself in the darkness, my face bloody and throbbing, and my soul crushed.

The weeks before Carrie died were some of the hardest. She was a completely different person, and it hurt beyond belief to feel as though I didn't know my own sister, much less my twin. Even after all these months, the pain of that day hit me just as hard. Reliving the memory had consumed most of my run, so before I knew it, I was near the clearing where the pond was. Although I wasn't a pro at running, I could go for longer and farther than I used to, and I often switched between running, jogging, and brisk walking. Would Carrie have been proud?

Chapter 17

When I had left my house, it was dark out. Now, the sun was rising, shedding beautiful pink, orange, yellow and red rays through the branches of the trees, a sight that took my breath away. Even when I was at my worst, the surprise of the beauty of nature managed to make me feel something other than pain. I stretched a moment before I took off at a run to reach the edge of the pond. I was quickly stopped in my tracks. So quickly, in fact, that I nearly took a tumble over a large branch in the middle of the path. Sitting on a thick log right at the edge of the water was a boy in a plaid flannel shirt, the edges of his hair curling just above the collar. His face was lifted directly towards the sun, his arms comfortably at his sides.

I didn't understand why Julian had to be everywhere I was, both in and out of my thoughts, but there was something about this moment that seemed fateful. Although Julian had odd sleeping habits, I was surprised to see him at such an early hour. With all of my heart, I wanted to walk up to the log, wrap my arms around him, and be held. It had been so long since I'd been comforted by anyone, and I ached to feel a pair of arms securing me.

Despite my yearning, I wasn't ready for the confrontation. I began to turn around, and as luck would have it, immediately tripped over the branch and fell face first into a pile of leaves. The yelp that came from my mouth combined with the crunch of the leaves made for a noise that couldn't be missed. Not only was I extremely awkward every time I saw Julian, but I must also look like the biggest klutz alive.

I lay still for a moment, desperately hoping that he somehow didn't hear the commotion. I didn't hear anything for a moment, so I thought somehow my prayers had been answered. Two seconds later, however, I felt a twig slowly being removed from my hair. Julian kneeled above me, his lips forming an expression that was at once amused and concerned. He held out his hand, offering me help. I, being the stubborn person I am, refused his hand and slowly sat up, wiping dirt off of my cheek.

Julian sighed before speaking. "When are you going to talk to me? I know things have changed. I know life is different now, but I don't think I deserve to be ignored forever."

"You don't," I answered softly, my throat feeling as though it were closing and my mouth suddenly becoming incredibly dry. "You deserve much better," I continued, "which is why I don't think we should be friends."

I regretted what I said before it was completely out of my mouth. His eyebrows rose in confusion, and he looked at me with eyes that were cloudy, flashing dark on a day that promised nothing. I stood up and brushed myself off before I ran away. It seemed it was all I did anymore.

I managed to make it home without crying. When I got there, the door was locked. I hadn't brought my key, and I hadn't counted on either of my parents being awake before I got home, so I'd foolishly left it unlocked. Angry at the way such a beautiful morning could turn sour, I kicked the door and pummeled it with my fists a couple times, instantly feeling the pain. It might have hurt, but it felt better than anything else I'd felt that day. I crumbled to the ground, leaning my head against the porch rails and wanting nothing more than to just disappear from the earth. Seconds later, the door opened.

My dad was immaculately groomed, his dark, wavy hair short and stylish, his complexion flawless and his blue eyes piercing. He was dressed in a charcoal suit in a slim cut tailored to perfection. As always, he looked like he should be in a magazine or in a movie, not a regular father. He was a lawyer. He had always been handsome, successful, and charming, but it was only in the last few months that he had been dressing with such care. He'd transformed into a cool, intimidating figure that I wasn't used to. Before, he'd come home and immediately change from his suit to jeans, clothes he could play with Grizzly in or swing his daughters around in. Now, he stayed in his suit and remained behind closed doors minutes after he walked in.

"Good morning," he boomed, his voice far more cheerful than it had been the other day. He flashed an awkward smile at me and gestured for me to come in. "Out for a run?" he asked casually, as if our confrontation never happened. I looked at him suspiciously but didn't answer, instead heading straight for the kitchen to drink a tall glass of cold water. Surprisingly, he followed me in there.

"Look, Felicia," he began, his voice slightly hesitant, "I'm sorry for the way I acted yesterday. If you have curiosity in my business, who am I to turn you away? You want to learn the ins and outs of law? You got it, kid!"

I looked at him as though he were insane and rinsed the cup before placing it in the sink. I couldn't believe he was trying to turn this around and convince me that I hadn't been searching for something deeper. Then again, he was a lawyer.

No one in the family had been this cheerful in the past year. I knew this was some kind of façade for me to stop bothering him, but I wouldn't let up that easy. Besides, Carrie had been the one who'd been interested in law. I wanted to become a powerful author, editor, and publisher--my version of a triple threat.

Was my father just trying to turn me into a version of Carrie so he didn't have to miss her as much? I steamed inside, ready to turn around and give him a piece of my mind before I stopped myself, realization setting in. Who was I to berate my father when I'd been trying to turn myself into Carrie?

A devious thought struck me as I slowly nodded my head at him. The closer I got to my father, the closer I got to discovering who his "client" was. With a pang in my stomach, I also realized that maybe, just maybe we could get back to where we used to be. It was an odd feeling, not knowing the parents you've known for seventeen years of life. A house that had been so lively, clean, and warm was now cold and silent. It's hard to expect normality after a death in the family, but the distance between us all still astounded me.

"Sure, Dad," I said. I flashed him a fake smile and ran upstairs. I still had about an hour before school and was feeling a small amount of fuzziness from the idea of bonding with my father. I decided to call Andrew. He picked up after four rings, and his voice sounded muffled and sleepy.

"'Lo?" I heard.

"Hi," I said casually, as if the last time we talked hadn't been months ago.

"Felicia?" he asked, sounding as if he were stifling a yawn.

"Yup," I responded. "How goes it out there in Iowa?"

"It's fine," he answered suspiciously. "Why are you calling? Is something wrong with Mom?"

"No! I just wanted to see how you were doing. Can't a sister and brother engage in some form of communication once in a while?"

"Sure," he said slowly, his voice slightly relieved. "How are things at home, anyway?"

"They're about the same. Mom is still locked in her room and Dad is still locked in his office. There's something weird, though…" I let my voice trail off. I didn't want to bother Andrew with my concerns about Dad. He was stressed enough as it was, double- majoring in pre-law and business because my father had pushed him so hard. "There's uh, something weird growing in the backyard," I finished lamely, unable to come up with anything better.

"Too bad the gardener lady can't fix it," Andrew said soberly. "Maybe you should try to drag her out there. Could be good for her."

"Yeah, I'll do that," I responded hurriedly. "Well, it was nice taking to you!" I hung up quickly and felt stupid, wondering why I'd called him in the first place. I had to face it. There really was no one for me to connect with anymore.

Chapter 18

Almost a month and a half had gone by and I'd failed at discovering anything about my father and his office 'mistress' as I liked to think of her. I felt somewhat thinner, but it still seemed like no matter how hard I tried, I just couldn't lose weight the way Carrie had. I turned my attention to the journal I'd started in honor of Carrie. I didn't write much about my feelings in there, but I did use it as a way to measure my food intake.

I was proud of the last few weeks. There had been the whole frozen dinner mishap, but at least I'd gotten rid of it. I felt guilty and ashamed when I thought of what I'd done, but I'd never felt such power and control in my life. Even though it was vile and repulsive, it gave me a thrill that I yearned for again. Still, I knew that I didn't want to go down that path again, so I was going to try hard to stick to the diet.

I was dreading it, but I knew it was time to look in the mirror again. I didn't expect to see much, but I was pleasantly surprised when I realized my stomach looked slightly smaller. I knew it was probably just the lack of food intake, but at least it was something. I frowned at my legs and arms, but I had hope.

Carrie had looked similar to me before all of her drastic changes, and we virtually had the same body, so I knew I could achieve the same results she'd gotten with her hard work. On that upbeat note, I put all of my energy into styling my hair in a Carrie-approved fashion, and even managed to forget my father, Julian, and the fat my body likely wouldn't shed for quite some time.

The rest of the month passed by in what seemed like a blur. The days dragged on, but when the weekends finally hit, I realized how quickly it actually went by. I'd made a few purchases over the last week and they were ones that I was happy with. My most beloved purchase was one that I wasn't necessarily proud of, but secretly overjoyed to have. I also had some guilt over it, as it technically wasn't a purchase.

I'd been in my living room doing sit-ups. I had the TV on for comfort, just so the house wasn't so quiet, and was absentmindedly paying attention. After a couple hours of alternating between exercising and lounging, I realized that commercials for diet fads were quite frequent, even on channels that primarily catered to children's television. I'd been on a strict diet of fruits, vegetables, and some whole grains and I'd been exercising every day, but it didn't seem as though I were losing any weight. I know it takes time, but I was extremely frustrated.

Earlier that day, I'd passed Julian in the hallway. He was with the same girl. As I stared openly at the two, I noticed that she had very long, thin legs. The way they looked in her motorcycle boots illustrated what I ultimately wanted to achieve. Even more jealous, I nearly took my head off as I turned and almost slammed into the open locker door next to me. I really needed to work on my coordination skills.

Thus, out of jealousy, frustration, and an impulsive and stupid idea to take the easy way out, I decided it was time to get some diet pills. I hopped on my bike and pedaled furiously to a grocery store that was out of my way--I couldn't risk running into Julian again. When I got there, I made a beeline for the nutrition section and found an entire wall of diet pills. After studying each one intently, I began to feel confused. There were so many different ingredients in each one and they all promised the same results. Finally, I made a decision based on quantity. One package had a 'buy one, get one free' deal, so I picked it up and walked excitedly to the self-checkout counter, reading the reviews on the back along the way. When I got there, the robotic voice blared, "Approval needed!"

An older woman with a kind smile walked over to me and asked for my ID. "What for?" I sputtered, unable to fathom why this would be going wrong for me.

"You have to be eighteen to buy diet pills. You really don't even need these, dear," she said, a concerned wrinkle in her forehead.

"I don't have my ID with me," I managed to choke out, fighting back tears. I dropped the bottle of pills and ran out the door, sobbing as I practically ripped the lock off my bike. I rode around for a few minutes, tears continuously streaming down my face. There was nothing I wanted more than those pills at this minute. I needed to lose weight! For a moment, a voice at the back of my head nagged me that I was acting like Carrie had in her last few weeks. I brushed it aside, positive that I wasn't and wouldn't ever get that crazy. Which is precisely why I made my brilliant next move.

I know it was incredibly stupid, selfish, and irresponsible, but I was desperate. I relocked my bike, went back into the store, and casually walked over to the nutrition section again. I studied the bottle for quite some time, and when no one was looking, pretended to check my phone, shoved the bottle into the bottom of my bag, and resumed studying the shelves. In an effort to look unsuspicious, I went through the checkout line and bought a bottle of water.

As I exited the store, my heart was beating so fast and loud, I was sure that everyone who was within a yard of me could hear it. At that moment, if someone even glanced at me, I felt the stare was accusing. Somehow, I made it outside without an alarm ringing, a salesperson stopping me, or a policeman tackling me. Instead of feeling a rush or relieved, I just felt sick to my stomach. I pulled a crumpled twenty out of my pocket and handed it to a cashier who was outside smoking. He looked startled and asked me what it was for. I couldn't exactly tell him I was stealing, so I quickly fabricated a story.

"One of your baggers accidentally put a couple bags in my cart earlier that must have been from a previous shopper. My parents wanted to make use of the items but we felt guilty taking them, so that should cover it. Thanks."

He shrugged and pocketed the money, giving me a lazy wave before sucking on his cigarette and turning away. My voice sounded high and unusually far as I spoke to him, and I felt cold all over. I walked to my bike and slowly got on, pedaling home with what should have been triumph but instead felt like failure.

71

Chapter 19

As days passed after the incident, it didn't affect me as much, but I knew it was definitely something I wasn't going to do again. Each day I took two pills and ate as little as possible, but I still wasn't seeing any results. Sunday night rolled around and I needed some inspiration from Carrie. I fell backwards onto the bed and reached underneath to pull out my source of contact. Hopefully this entry would be more upbeat than the last.

Things have been decent lately. I've managed to go quite a few days without eating and even received some compliments from my "friends." Whatever they see, I don't. As cliché as it sounds, I look in the mirror and still see the same person that was there months ago. My parents and people at school have started to tell me that I look too skinny, but honestly, I think I could stand to lose a lot more weight--at least twenty pounds. I need to figure out something to keep my energy up, because I had a scare this morning. I was taking a shower and suddenly everything went black. I fell forward and hit my head on the wall and nearly lost my balance and fell out of the bathtub. This seems like the perfect sign for me to stop trying to lose weight, but I don't want to. I don't want to and I can't. Dad brought home hot dogs from my absolute favorite restaurant today, and instead of being tempted, I was repulsed. So literally, I can't. Things are changing in my body, and it's happening without my consent. I never feel warm anymore, even when I wear two sweatshirts to sleep in and bundle up in my thick comforters. When I was brushing my hair this morning, a small clump the size of a quarter came out, and it terrified me. Odd bruises show up on my body even though I haven't bumped into anything lately, and the complexion of my face is pasty. I guess I can expect minor setbacks, but nothing will stop me from getting where I want to be.

My hands were shaking when I finished reading the entry. I had never known that such terrible things had been happening to Carrie. Even when she began to look sickly, she always managed to put on a face that was optimistic. I immediately felt guilty. There I was, traipsing around without a care in the world while she was suffering.

Once again, I was struck by the lack of connection we had. We were twins. Wasn't I supposed to get some sort of twin instinct that something was wrong? I had to be the worst sister ever. In that moment, Julian and my father seemed far away. The only thing that was important to me was living for Carrie. Carrie was disgusted by body fat, and I would not disgust her. I would continue on my journey to be just like her—to become her.

A few days later, I woke up and nearly fell out of my bed—partly from fear and partly from surprise. A pair of steely gray eyes stared down at me, hard yet unsure. My father managed an awkward smile and placed his large hand on my shoulder.

"Hey, kiddo. Ready to study some law?" he asked in an attempt to be enthusiastic but instead sounding somewhat forced.

I reached up and rubbed the sleep from my eyes, confused at the disturbing way I'd been woken up. It took a moment to realize it was Saturday, and when I glanced at the clock, I realized it wasn't even eight in the morning yet. I rolled over and groaned, hoping that would be enough to send my father away, but he wasn't shaken.

He timidly sat on the edge of my bed, an odd sight for me to see. When I was younger, my father used to slam his hands down on the bed to wake us up. The move would send us flying and we'd giggle in glee, glad to go downstairs and be his assistants while he whisked eggs, milk, and cinnamon to make French toast. Now he was afraid to sit on my bed? My suspicions about him rose and I felt annoyed with him for ruining my morning, especially a morning that I hadn't planned on being awake for.

The scent of sugar and warm dough roused me from beneath the covers. It was a habit I hadn't quite shaken, and I wasn't proud of it. My father held a small plate of donuts under my nose, complete with a dish of creamy, sweet dipping sauce. The donuts were warm and flaky, crispy and sugary on the outside with a thick, rich and crumby texture inside.

They had been a Saturday morning staple at a time. While we didn't get them every single week, when we did, we knew it would be a special day. The tantalizing sugary aroma would make its way up to our rooms, tempting us out of our beds. When those donuts were on the table, everything was pleasant. No one fought over them because the basket seemed never-ending. Once the small white dish towel that held the donuts began to become visible with its spots of grease, I'd turn away for one second and it'd be filled again. Wide smiles would flash around the table, everyone happily munching the sweet treats.

My dad hadn't made these donuts in over a year. The rich scent didn't fill the house the way it once did, and I knew it was because it was far emptier now. Anger welled up inside of me. It's not as though I expected my father to understand, but I almost felt betrayed by the fact he'd brought these donuts to me when I was doing so well.

In one swift move, I brought my hand down on the dish and knocked the donuts to the floor. They rolled off the plate and onto my floor, leaving a small trail of powdered sugar and grease behind. My father stared at me in shock, his eyes narrowing. I could sense anger bubbling up inside of him, but he reacted calmly. He wiped his hands on the sides of his pants and slowly got up from the bed.

"Meet me in my office in twenty minutes. Approximately."

He was gone in a flash, his trim body moving sleekly and quickly as a cat, often exiting and rarely entering. I was left with my worst enemy. It was a stare-off between me and the donuts, and they looked as if they were winning. The sunlight streamed through the window and reflected off of them, giving them a golden shine that made them appear almost heavenly, like celestial creatures. I'd have given anything in that moment to sink my teeth into one of those soft, delicious fried concoctions, but I knew I'd regret it.

Instead, I whisked them up onto the plate, whipped myself over to the window, and threw them down into the grass before I could think about it. I knew my father would be annoyed when he'd cut the grass the next day, but I'd come really close to blowing it. I'd done well for the last week, sticking to a diet of fruits and vegetables and drinking only water. The scale said that I'd lost five pounds, but the mirror disagreed, so I had to keep at it.

After washing my face and brushing my teeth, I stalked back to my room to change out of my pajamas. I was tempted to stay in them to tick my father off, as he loathed unprofessionalism, but I remember how Carrie would walk into his office wearing pinstriped pants, a grey cashmere sweater, and pearl earrings. I didn't want to give into his need for neatness and proper appearance, but I reminded myself that this wasn't for him, but for Carrie.

I strode into his office four minutes early and confident. I didn't bother knocking as I wanted to make a glamorous entrance, carrying a legal pad in my hand and wearing a watch that had never been worn before on my wrist. I'd figured it'd make me look important, as though I had places to be and things to do.

Unfortunately, I seemed to have walked in at the wrong time. My father held the phone close to his ear, a dreamy smile on his face. He appeared to be cooing into the phone, as if he were talking to a baby. Once he heard me come in, he nearly dropped the phone. His cheeks took on a slight blush and he cleared his throat, taking a moment to regain his composure.

"Yes. The documents will be mailed this afternoon and should arrive by Monday," he spoke into the phone gruffly.

He hung up quickly and forced a smile, his normally bright eyes dull and lacking emotion. I noticed for the first time that despite the tired eyes, the rest of him looked even more put together than usual. Only a couple weeks ago I'd thought he looked terrible. Now, his thick hair looked shiny and was cut in a trendy style. His figure wasn't as thin as it had been, but rather slightly muscular. Even his skin seemed tanner and healthier.

It was odd. For a moment, I felt resentful that my normally beautiful mother was so unkempt. Clearly, my father wasn't too depressed to hit the...tanning salon? Very, very odd. My hackles rose and my lips instantly pursed in disapproval as I shot my father a cool glance. He ignored me and clasped his hands together, offering a smile.

"Let's get started!" he encouraged, passing me an introductory law book. I took it and slid it underneath my legal pad, glancing around his office for any clues. I saw nothing out of the ordinary and realized that I'd have to find a way to get in here when he wasn't home. I flashed him a fake smile.

"Do you think I could have a key to your office, Dad…dy?" I asked sweetly, trying not to sound awkward. "I really think it would help me get a sense of what it's like to be in a lawyer's environment."

"Well, sweetheart," he chuckled, "We'd have to get you in the courtroom for that! But if you wanted to come in here to do work once in a while, I don't see why it'd be a problem. I'll leave the door unlocked from now on."

I frowned. This was too easy. Why was he being so agreeable? He took my furrowed brow as a sign that I was ready to start studying and began droning on and on about politics and law. I pretended to jot sentences down every now and then, but it made me sick to my stomach to be in the room with him. I prayed that he wasn't doing what I suspected him of doing, but it all seemed to match up too perfectly.

I distracted myself with thoughts of walking through the school doors in a sleek outfit, my figure lean and model-esque. I would walk confidently down the hall and shoot a penetrating glare at Locker Girl, who would crumble at my feet and bow to the name of fashion. My father mistook my sudden smile for pleasure in the lecture and roused me from my daydream.

"I can't tell you how glad I am that you're into this, Fee," he said.

My nose wrinkled at the nickname he hadn't used in months, but I forced a smile and responded, "Yeah, law is…totally cool! Thanks, Dad."

Chapter 20

Later that evening, I lay on my floor while doing bicycle kicks in the air. The evening was quiet, as it always was, and I was waiting for the light down the hallway to go off. When it did and I heard the click of the television being turned on and the gentle hum of noise, I shot up like a ninja and rolled my way over to my door.

I opened it a crack and peeked through to make sure the coast was clear. When I determined it was, I stealthily crept down the hallway until I reached my father's office. Grizzly suddenly padded over to me, his heavy breathing sounding louder than ever. I held a finger to my lips. My dog must be smart, because he got the gesture and he sat down silently. When I turned the knob, I was surprised that the door instantly gave. I honestly hadn't expected my father to have kept it unlocked.

I'd brought a small flashlight with me so I wouldn't have to risk turning on the light and waking anyone up. It felt weird being in here alone. I sank into his plush, leather seat and swiveled as I looked around. This was my father's special place, a space he had spent years building into his dream room. His walls were covered in diplomas and photographs, and his desk and drawers were filled with important legal documents. A flat-screen television hung in the corner and a small mini-fridge sat beside his desk, stocked with bottled water, fruit, gelatin, and the occasional beer.

For years, he'd come here to get away. If Carrie and I were arguing, if Andrew was practicing his guitar, or if my mom was on the phone with her sister, Dad would come up here and lock the door, lean back, and watch football on high blast. It was a sanctuary where everything that was important to him surrounded him. When I finally stopped spinning, my eyes landed on the computer. My heart stopped for a moment and my jaw hung open in shock.

Ever since I can remember, the space next to my father's computer had been occupied by a large silver frame. It was engraved in elegant script adorned with vines and proclaimed, "World's Best Dad!" The photograph that filled the frame featured me, Carrie, Andrew, my parents, and Grizzly. We all stood in front of the peach tree in the backyard. My parents had their hands on our shoulders and Grizzly, only a puppy, nestled at our feet.

The day the picture had been taken was absolutely beautiful. It was late spring and the sun was bright in the sky, casting a glow on our faces that made us look angelic. White and pink flowers swirled in the background and our grins were wide, like nothing bad had ever happened to us and nothing could touch us. It had been everyone's favorite picture. I remember coming into my father's office as a child and sitting on his lap on the chair, always looking at the picture and thinking about how familiar and safe it was, a memento that stayed in one spot and would always be there.

That goes to show how naïve children are. The picture was gone, and I couldn't believe it. It took only a minute before a strangled, guttural moan rose up from my stomach. Before I could stop myself, I had swept everything off of my father's desk. Papers, folders, pens, and office supplies littered the floor. Rage sent a shock to my heart, and I was desperate to find the picture. I opened the drawer of his desk and rifled through its contents but slammed it shut as hard as I could when I came up short. I went to his file cabinet and yanked on the handle but it wouldn't budge. He had it locked. I slammed my hands on the drawer in frustration and stepped back when it swayed and rumbled against the wall.

Giving up, I gazed around the cluttered room and sighed. The office, ordinarily immaculate, looked as though a tornado had run through it. If this had happened a year before, I would have been terrified at the repercussions of getting caught. Today, I just sneered at the mess and decided to leave it. There was no way my father could hurt me any longer. His file cabinet wasn't the only thing that was going to stay locked.

Chapter 21

Days went by and my father hadn't said a word to me. I was surprised, but I was also relieved. At least I was off the hook with the stupid law study sessions. Besides, I had more important things to worry about. I was doing really well with my diet.

That week, I'd consumed little more than fruits, vegetables, and water. When I realized how expensive eating healthy was, I just cut some of my portions and was rewarded with an even smaller calorie total. I'd begun to write down every single morsel I put into my mouth and was really pleased when they added up to less than 1000 calories. I'd made it to school, but it hadn't been easy to concentrate when I was so engrossed with my eating plans. The good news, though, was that I barely had time to think about Julian.

When the bell rang at the end of the day, I nearly ran out of the classroom. I couldn't wait to get home and start my crunches. I'd decided to increase them by twenty-five every week. So far I was up to 200 a night, and I could feel that my jeans were a little looser around my waist. They were still too tight around my thighs, but there was no greater euphoria than the one I received when my jeans slid down a little.

After tossing my books into my locker and slamming it shut, I whirled around and being the clumsy person I am, walked directly into someone's hard chest. Knowing that it would be Julian with my luck, I prepared myself to tell him that I wasn't interested in trying to keep the friendship. Yes, it was going to hurt both of us immensely, but I just couldn't face him after all I'd done to him. I composed myself and lifted my chin.

"Look," I started, before realizing I was gazing up into two green orbs framed by long, thick lashes that looked as though they belonged in a mascara commercial. Peach lips curved into a smile, revealing teeth as straight and white as a row of Chiclets. A perfectly chiseled jaw and straight nose only added to the perfection. Chestnut brown hair was artfully arranged in stylish waves. He had clear, pale skin, so white that the permanent pink splotches on his cheekbones stood out, making him even more boyish and adorable. The only source of imperfection on his entire face was a small scar in his right eyebrow, but it only served to add intrigue to his profile. Joshua Avalos. The school's very own Adonis.

"Felicia," his deep voice started. "Are you okay?"

I almost laughed at the absurdity of it all, but I wasn't going to be rude to him. He'd been Carrie's boyfriend's best friend, and he'd even had a thing with Carrie at the beginning of freshman year. He'd always been nice to me, and even though he hung out with girls who made fun of me, he'd never joined in. Whenever I had to be around him, he went out of his way to make me feel welcome, unlike the rest of the group. I knew, however, that he really didn't care; he was just raised to be a polite boy.

He was a member of just about every sports team in school and president of the debate club. He was kind, honest, and thoughtful, and just about every girl in the school was in love with him. I was immune to his charm and had often made fun of him with Julian. We'd call him the All-American boy and began humming the Star Spangled Banner when he was near.

"I'm fine," I answered slowly, and bent down to pick up the rest of my books.

"Let me get that," he replied, kneeling down to gather them up. While he was on the floor, I awkwardly stood there, my cheeks burning in embarrassment. Wanting to look anywhere but the site of my most recent moment of klutziness, I turned my gaze to the right and looked directly into the eyes of Julian.

He stood across the hall with his locker lady at his side. She wore olive shorts, a white lace blouse, and purple flat shoes. She appeared to be speaking to him, but his gaze was fixed on me, and his eyes burned with curiosity and something else I couldn't detect. His mouth was set in a deep frown. I realized that it must appear that I was talking to Josh, and he didn't seem to like it. Locker Girl waved her hand in front of his face and followed his stare, realizing he was looking at me. She raised her eyebrow but offered me a small smile, and finally, Julian turned back to her and replied, but the frown didn't leave his face.

When Josh finally lifted his tall, lean-muscled body from the floor (what had he been doing down there anyway?), I snatched my books out of his hands and mumbled a quick "thank you" before taking off.

When the bus pulled up, I climbed on and made my way to the back to sit down. A small scrap of paper fluttered to the floor from one of my notebooks, but I didn't pay much attention to it. I hadn't been taking notes in school since I'd been so preoccupied, so I knew it couldn't be too important. A small, elderly woman next to me reached down and picked it up, handing it to me with a kind smile. I thanked her and turned it over in my hands, amazed at what I saw.

Josh's name and number was scrawled messily in bold black writing, the letters jagged and rising out of the paper's lines. I was infuriated. Who did he think he was? Josh dated girls that wore heels that clicked down the hall annoyingly. Their voices were high-pitched, bubbly, and traveled through classrooms so that the entire school could hear what they were talking about. Their skirts were short, their hair was processed, and their skin was baked. I certainly didn't fit the criteria.

I was probably just something exotic to him, the girl that dressed differently and read a book, not *US Weekly*. Or maybe his friends had made a bet with him to date the dorkiest person he could find. Perhaps his kindness made him see me as a charity case. Either way, he wasn't going to get a call from me. I wanted to crumple up the piece of paper and toss it out the window, but instead, I found myself smoothing it out and placing it back in my notebook. At that moment, the bus hit a pothole and everything went black for a second. My body grew hot, my head felt dizzy, and my mouth tasted like it was full of copper. I shook my head and snapped out of it, but it really frightened me.

The only time I'd ever felt like that before was when I'd spent a hot day at the amusement park and hadn't ate or drank much and was dehydrated. I rooted around my backpack for a bottle of water and chugged half of it, figuring Carrie's plan would work. It did, and a moment later, I felt fine again, but I couldn't shake the nagging feeling that something was wrong.

Chapter 22

Around ten, I'd done my crunches, eaten some chopped celery and sliced apples, and spent about an hour jogging. I was lying flat on my stomach on the floor, flipping through last year's yearbook. My food journal, which was also dubbed the 'Carrie Notebook' now not only held my food recordings, but notes on how I could become more like Carrie.

There were plenty of pictures of her in the yearbook, and she seemed to have been the best at everything. An entire page was devoted to her and her boyfriend, Peter, as the cutest couple. Peter was over 6 feet tall, had short dark blonde hair, a muscular body, and elfin yet elegant features. He was right beside Josh on the list of the school's most desirable.

In the first picture on the page, Carrie looked normal and happy. She was of an average size, on the thin side, and had her arms wrapped around Peter with a huge smile on her face. In the last picture, she looked incredibly scrawny. Her clothes seemed to hang on her, and her collarbone jutted out in a way that wasn't really attractive. Her legs looked like two sticks of linguine, and it appeared as though Peter could wrap one hand around her entire waist. She was smiling in the photo, but her eyes looked glazed and distant. Peter stared down at her with a grin on his face, but his eyes looked worried and just as far away as hers.

A spooky sensation came over me. It was odd seeing Carrie's photos that weren't perfect, because they usually were. I continued to look through the pages, and finally came to Josh's photo. Julian was on the page next to it. They were both so beautiful, but in extremely different ways. Julian's eyes were haunting, and his bone structure was delicate, suggesting he came from a different era. Josh's eyes were more welcoming, but they were full of mystery and intrigue. His smirk suggested that everything was not as it appeared, while Julian's somber expression portrayed him as someone who was mourning something.

Josh's number was on the floor next to the yearbook, and I picked it up, running my fingers over his name. I knew that I didn't particularly care for him, but in that moment, all I could think about was Julian and his Locker Girl. I know it was unfair, especially since I was the one who'd stopped talking to him, but I couldn't help feeling as though he'd abandoned me. We'd been such good friends, and I suppose part of me wanted him to fight for me, even though another part wished he would never try. Josh was who Carrie was. Maybe talking to him could actually help me to get closer to my goal. After nearly an hour of holding the paper and dialing and hanging up before it connected, I finally decided to call him. It rang three times before he picked it up.

"Hello?" he answered, his voice smooth and almost deeper on the phone than it was in person. "Hello?" he asked again, making me realize I hadn't said anything.

"Um, hi!" I blurted out, the state of my voice giving away my nervousness. "It's, um, Felicia. I found your number in my notebook, and I was just calling…"

"Felicia," he said warmly, sounding as if he was genuinely glad to hear from me. "How are you? It was weird running into you today. I feel like I haven't seen you in forever, and I just wanted to see what you've been up to."

Too polite. If this was Julian, we'd have been cracking stupid jokes by now and ignoring each other while he played the guitar and I wrote poetry. We'd sat on the phone for hours, each of us doing out own thing but there to listen to one another, and even if we weren't talking, it was nice just having each other's company. I reminded myself that this was not Julian, nor was I looking for a replacement for Julian.

"That's really nice of you to ask. I'm doing okay, thanks."

He let out a small chuckle that sounded nervous before replying. "You know, it's weird. When I ran into you in the hallway, you looked so much like Carrie, I was just in shock. I think that's why I stopped for so long."

I remained silent for a moment, knowing that it would probably make him uncomfortable but unable to come up with a quick response. It had been quite a while since someone my age had said something to me about Carrie. It had been quite a while since anyone had, really, even my parents. But it seemed as though a small pick had begun chipping away at the ice that was formed around my heart, and I felt a warmth that I hadn't felt in quite some time. All I'd been trying to do the past month was get closer to Carrie, and finally someone had recognized it!

"Thanks, Josh. That's really sweet of you to say and it means a lot."

After that, the conversation somehow seemed to flow naturally. We were on the phone for nearly an hour, talking about everything from music to literature to his football games. I'd spent the last few minutes in complete surprise, unable to believe that he was into some bands that I'd have never figured he'd heard of, and even more surprised when he claimed he was a Beats fan. I almost felt ashamed, realizing that I was just as guilty of judging people as I assumed they were of judging me. He really was someone different underneath that model exterior. When we finally hung up, I had agreed to meet him for pizza on Friday night.

I fell back onto my bed with a dramatic sigh, mocking the clichéd scene from television shows and movies that pictured girls arriving home from their first dates. I snorted at the silliness of it all and climbed under my comforter, ready for bed with a smile, something that seemed foreign to me. I slowly drifted off into a sleep-like state, only to shoot up in horror when I'd realized that meeting him for pizza meant I actually had to eat the pizza.

Never in my life had the idea of pizza seemed like a bad thing, but I knew I'd be paying for this. The whole week would have to be spent limiting my intake and working out. I wasn't even sure it was worth it. But after assuring myself that this was something Carrie did all the time, I managed to fall asleep soundly. Finally, I was branching outside the familiar. Finally, I too had become someone.

Chapter 23

The next night, Josh called me. I was surprised, but pleasantly so. We'd been talking for nearly an hour when the call-waiting beeped. Flushed with pleasure from the conversation, I clicked over without checking the ID, figuring it was a telemarketer anyway.

"Hello?" I chirped brightly, ready to say, "No thanks!"

"Felicia," a sad voice stated, familiar and distant all at once. "I really would like to talk to you at some point. It's not fair to do this to me, to do this to us."

"Julian, what us? We were friends in high school. Friends don't always stay friends forever. Now if you'll excuse me, I'm on the other line." I couldn't believe how mean I sounded, but I was still upset that he'd found a replacement for me so quickly and still embarrassed at my behavior.

"With who? Avalos?" he growled.

"It's not your business, but as a matter of fact, yes," I replied, standing on my tiptoes and twirling around in front of the mirror, liking that an old shirt that used to be tight on me hung near my stomach, neck, and shoulders.

"Meet me in front of the tree in an hour," he pleaded with a sense of urgency.

Before I could answer, he'd hung up. My heart dropped to my stomach, unable to believe that after being apart for so long, he still wanted to reunite. It took a moment until I remembered that I was still on the phone with Josh, and I clicked over in a slight daze.

"Sorry," I said.

"Hey, that's okay. Were you trying on outfits for our date Friday?" he asked teasingly.

It was so ridiculously cheesy that I couldn't help but smile. I liked that Josh had the ability to make me laugh, and I liked that I was finding out things about him that I'd never known before. He did have intelligence, he was interesting, and he could carry on a conversation.

I don't know why I'd always thought he was so dumb before, but the real Josh was nothing like the person I'd imagined. Part of me wondered if I was forcing myself to find reasons to like him because of my 'Becoming Carrie' plan, but for the most part, I was just surprised that I'd found someone I'd actually liked. I talked to him for another twenty minutes and hung up the phone, sitting on the edge of my bed and wringing my hands.

I wanted to go meet Julian, but I was afraid of what would happen. As much as I wanted to rub a magic lamp and wish the last year away, I knew that would never happen. Some sort of confrontation was going to take place, and I just wasn't ready for it. At the same time, I didn't have the heart to blow Julian off.

I could picture him standing in front of the tree, the breeze rustling his dark hair and his eyes large and worried, bright against his pale skin. He'd be wrapped in a black hooded sweatshirt and slim-fitting jeans, jeans that Peter and his friends used to make fun of before they suddenly became fashionable last year. When I thought of that, I felt a twinge, remembering just how different our groups were. With that, I'd made up my mind to meet him. Even if I didn't necessarily think we should stay friends, I owed him that much.

I stomped to the closet and yanked on a black hooded sweatshirt and black yoga pants. My hair tumbled down my back in knots, but I didn't bother to run a brush through it. I glanced at myself in the mirror, noticing that I looked tired but knowing there wasn't much I could do about it. Slipping on a pair of old moccasins, I walked into the hallways and slid quietly past my father's office, noticing the light was on. I listened intensely, but I could only hear a faint tapping of keys. Giving up, I crept down the stairs and opened the door, walking out into the cool evening.

The streetlights were out and the moon wasn't very bright, so there was no glow cast upon me as I walked to the old park. It was slightly spooky, but I hummed to myself and kept my hands shoved in my pockets, ready to break into a run if need be. The wind howled and leaves danced on the ground, a perfect accompaniment to the chilling evening.

When I finally reached the park's entrance, I saw a tall figure slouched against the tree. I could tell it was Julian simply by the way he stood. As he continued to grow, he began to slouch because he felt uncomfortable being so much taller than everyone else. I'd always chided him for it, finding it ridiculous that he felt the need to do that, but he'd constantly tell me that he wanted to be on the same level as everyone else. He'd felt it was more fair, which didn't make much sense to me, but Julian was very into the idea of fairness and forgiveness, two concepts I probably wouldn't be using tonight.

The moonlight fell upon him in a way that made his pale face seem to glow, almost as if he were supernatural. The wind whipped his dark hair against his cheeks, pink from the cold, and it was a beautiful contrast. I cursed myself for thinking that, but it wasn't something I could deny. His features were so sharp and delicate, it was almost as though he belonged in a painting from another century. Dressed in his usual black, there was something elegantly spooky about his appearance, conjuring images of vampires.

I laughed at my own silliness, knowing I'd never get sucked into that trend (no pun intended), but I did see the intrigue. As I finally reached him, I realized how fast my heart was pounding, and I started biting my nails just to have something to do. He looked up in surprise, his eyebrows rising and relief washing over his face.

He said nothing. Lifting his back from up against the tree, he simply stood straight and held out his arms. Every part of my body struggled to stay still, but it had been so long since I'd been hugged or comforted, so long since I'd been a part of Julian's life, and so long since I'd felt wanted by anyone that I ran to them, feeling a warmth that I hadn't experienced in months. We stood like that for several minutes in silence. My cheek rested against his arm, the fabric of his sweater soft on my skin. If anyone happened to be walking by, they'd see two uneven dark figures bathed in the pale moonlight that had suddenly made an appearance.

As good as the reunion felt, I knew it couldn't last. I slowly untangled myself from his arms and stepped back, forcing myself to look up at him. Tonight, his eyes were a deep hazel, flecks of green vibrant against the amber tones. He looked confused and worried, and I was sorry that I wouldn't be able to do anything to appease him.

"Julian, as much as I miss you, we both know that things aren't the same anymore," I said quietly, only able to hold his gaze for so long before my eyes met the grass.

"I don't believe you," he replied, shoving his hands in his pockets and kicking at a pile of twigs near the tree. "Sometimes, I think I know you better than you know yourself, and right now, I know that you need me in your life."

"No," I said firmly, taken aback by his unexpected boldness. "I don't. I have too many things to concentrate on, and they don't include you."

There I went again, being harsh as possible. I winced and realized I needed to take it down a notch. "

That is to say, I'm really busy lately, and I'll admit, I'm embarrassed by the way things ended for us, so I really just can't imagine trying to take up where we left off."

Julian grabbed me by the arms and bent down so that he was eye level with me. He was so close, I could almost see his pores, see every inch of perfectly clear skin, and see each long, dark individual eyelash.

"You. Don't. Get. It," he spat, emphasizing each word as though I were too obtuse to understand, which I suppose I was. "I love you, Felicia."

The words hung in the air between us, changing the environment and making everything suddenly far too awkward.

"As a friend!" he quickly added, seeing the error of his word choice. I could sense his pain and watched myself moving back from the reflection in his eyes

. "You mean everything to me. We've been through so much together, and we've always been there for each other. You can't deny what we had as friends! Never have I been so close to someone in my life." He spoke hurriedly, his words running over each other in a desperate attempt to fill the gap that was becoming wider between us.

I couldn't speak at that moment, couldn't breathe. My chest tightened and my lungs felt constricted, almost as though someone was pushing down on my ribcage, trying to take away all ability to breathe. That's when everything changed.

Chapter 24

In an instant, I fully morphed into Carrie. Although she was never too mean to anyone, she didn't take comments that she didn't agree with lightly. She was nice to Julian when he was around, but at home, she constantly nagged at me for hanging out with him. One particular night, she spilled feelings to me that changed the way we spoke to each other from then on.

"I just don't get it, Fee," she said in a bored tone, yanking a brush through her long, unruly locks.

"No offense, but Julian is kind of a geek. I mean, he totally tripped over his own feet in the library today and his books went flying. One of them hit Kassie in the head!"

I stifled a giggle, thinking about how funny that must have been. Kassie's over-processed, fried hair was indestructible, so I'm sure she wasn't hurt too badly.

Carrie whipped around and shot daggers from her eyes.

"This isn't funny, Felicia," she remarked coldly. "He's always throwing off the curve in Algebra and making everyone get lousy grades! And he just always has to raise his hand and argue with whatever anyone else says. Don't even get me started on his wardrobe. His pants are so tight that I'm surprised he can ever get himself out of them, and I sincerely doubt that he will be able to have children in the future. And the way you two sit upside down on the couch and throw popcorn at each other like you're animals or something—it's just disgusting!"

"Are you done with your monologue?" I yawned. I flipped my feet over the side of the bed and sat up to look at her, but she was too busy doing leg lifts to look back. "First of all, I can't help it that your class is full of idiots who aren't willing to study. Julian is not responsible for your friends' grades, and he shouldn't have to limit his intelligence to appease your cronies! And last time I checked, Julian and I throwing popcorn at each other is a little more entertaining and a little less gross than watching you and Peter shove your tongues down each other's throats!"

She'd sniffed at my retort, turning away to look at the mirror. She was incredibly thin, made obvious by her clothes. Her leggings, which were supposed to cling everywhere, were loose around her knees, making for an odd appearance. Her shirt had to have been a size small, but in bunched up around her shoulders and billowed out around her midsection when it had previously taken to her shape.

"I really just think that it would be better for m—your image if you tried to meet new people," she said, scrunching her nose as she pinched imaginary pieces of fat at her midsection.

At that point, I'd gotten angry. "Julian has been nothing but nice to you! How could you say such terrible things about him?"

She'd looked at me coolly and without remorse. "When you're me, you have the opportunity to pick and choose. But if you don't choose right the first time around, you're done," she'd replied matter-of-factly, resuming her exercise and ignoring me for the rest of the night.

In my effort to be Carrie, I was determined to make this flawless. I stood straight and put my hands on my hips, eyes narrowed and looking at him directly.

"Julian, you need to give this up already," I said bossily, channeling Carrie at her meanest. "We were friends; now we aren't. I am pretty sure that you of all people are capable of understanding such a simple problem." I even added in a good neck roll for quick measure, and pursed my lips as I stared him down in defiance.

His features grew puzzled and his face slowly clouded into a full-blown storm. His complexion almost looked like a watercolor mood mural, changing slowly from pale white to sickly grey to angry rouge. His hands clenched at his side and he drew himself up to his full height, towering over me almost menacingly. I braced myself for the impact of his verbal blow, expecting it to be loud, confrontational, and filled with spite. Instead, he spoke quietly and simply, almost as if he were just delivering news.

"As hard as you seem to be trying to get me away from you, it hasn't been working. But you can rest assured that you're finally driving me away. Will you be able to sleep tonight?"

We were both silent for a moment, and my heart clenched, and my stomach felt as though a giant avocado pit had lodged itself right in the middle, forcing me to grab it in pain. Apparently, I could dish it out, but I didn't handle taking it too well. The wind blew, leaves fell from the trees, and a dog barked in the distance, but the expression on Julian's face didn't change as he resumed speaking.

"It's apparent that I don't know who you are anymore, but the real question is: do you?"

I began to interject, but he cut me off, somehow knowing exactly what I was going to say.

"This isn't about a few clothing choices," he continued. "You're just...not nice anymore. And honestly, I'm concerned about your health. You look like you stopped eating."

For a moment, my head swelled with pride, and then I realized that it wasn't a compliment in Julian's eyes. However, despite its falsity, it was probably one of the greatest things I'd heard all day, and for the moment, I was able to feel okay about myself. A smile played at the corner of my lips, almost a smirk, and it was simply from the absentmindedness at being told that someone, *someone* had noticed I'd lost weight, but Julian mistook it for me finding something funny.

He threw his hands up in the air and gave me one last glance, and his eyes were icier than I'd ever seen them before. The warmth had been replaced with a dull gray that shined like evening snow on the tip of a glacier. Stonily, he said, "I give up," and walked briskly from the tree, taking not only himself but everything that was ever important to me with him.

Chapter 25

Although I'd felt comfortable before, I instantly went cold. All feeling seemed to drain from my body, and I'd never felt as empty as I did in that moment. This was a different kind of emptiness from the way I felt with Carrie, and as horrible as it sounded, all I could think about was how lost I felt, but how that was a good thing because I knew for sure I wouldn't eat that night.

I put my head down and thrust my hands deep into the pockets of my hoodie, preparing myself for the long, sad journey home. I lifted my head to brush a tear that was beginning to fall from the corners of my eyes, but scolded myself, knowing that Carrie wouldn't have cried at a moment like this. As I looked up, I was surprised to see a tall, familiar figure striding towards me. He walked with purpose, and it almost looked as though he wasn't going to stop and would simply barrel into me and keep going.

I titled my chin up and tried to compose myself, opening my mouth to let him know that whatever he had to say wasn't going to matter since I no longer cared, since he no longer cared enough to keep trying. I know that it was selfish and childish to expect him to come after me even after I told him to quit, but I needed him to do that. Fearing the worst, I decided to throw a random insult out so I could beat him to whatever he had to say.

My moment was ceased as he swooped in, grabbed me by my arms, and leaned in. His body met mine in a perfect angle and seemingly out of nowhere, he crushed my lips with his, tasting of the fresh smoothies he made every day after work for a protein boost. The strawberry-soaked kiss was one I felt from my head to my toes, and even though there was something about it that felt like I was home, I convinced myself it was wrong.

I know that a lot of books and movies feature that moment where a girl and a boy kiss and it just feels 'right,' a cliché that I usually despise. For the first time ever, I realized it was true, but I couldn't possibly hurt Julian any more than I already was. Desperately trying to keep from crying, I bit my lip so hard that I nearly drew blood. I was exhausted, tired of repeating myself to him over and over, so I shielded my eyes from his gaze, kicked up my heels, and ran faster than I'd ever run before, not bothering to look back to see the hurt on his face.

The next day at school, I traveled the hallways with my head down, figuring it would be nearly impossible to avoid Julian but vowing to do my best. As I neared his locker, I caught site of a sweet pair of lace-up maroon combat boots and couldn't help myself from glancing up, jealous yet again of Locker Girl's wardrobe, bitter that she could dress so freely. She stood at Julian's locker with her notebooks pressed against her chest, turning her head every so often to search the hallway, a worried look on her face.

I felt smug for a moment, a touch of satisfaction knocking at my heart. Despite her looks, incredible style, and mystique, Julian had chosen to kiss me! Her eyes met mine, and she gave me an odd look as I passed, one that held both suspicion and curiosity in her eyes. I quickly looked away and continued walking.

The week continued much the same way. I'd pass Julian's locker, nonchalantly lift my head, and find her standing there without him. A pang struck my stomach, knowing that I was responsible for his missed absences. Julian and I had been the most intelligent kids in our grade, and I'd already lost my GPA after Carrie. I didn't want him to lose his, too. I decided that if he wasn't there the next day, I'd do something about it.

When I got home that night, I flipped through the pages of my food journal, noting that I'd done fairly well for the week. Trying to avoid thinking about Julian or my father really distracted me enough so that I didn't constantly have the urge to eat. I hadn't spoken to my father once. He left before I woke up, and his office door was shut whenever I got home. I tried opening it once in the middle of the night and was surprised to find that it was still unlocked. I planned on searching for the key to that drawer sometime this week, but for now, I was preoccupied with my date with Josh the next evening.

I knew something was wrong with me when I realized how terrified I was that I was going to have to eat pizza. Once a favorite food of mine, I couldn't imagine eating it now. All of the carbs! The grease! I shuddered just thinking about it. I'd spent a lot of time researching foods and their calorie contents on the Internet, and I couldn't believe what terrible things I used to eat. I'd been eating a lot of fruits and vegetables, but I was still disappointed when I looked in the mirror. I didn't expect instantaneous results, but it seemed like Carrie went from fit and healthy to pin-thin in a matter of days. Everything always was easy for her, so I don't know why I bother comparing. Things were going to be easy for me now, too.

Chapter 26

As I got ready for school the next morning, my stomach fluttered nervously. As someone who used to feel superior to Josh and his minions, I don't know why I was making such a big deal out of it. Even though our date wasn't until the evening, I still felt that the day revolved around it, so I wanted to look nice at school.

I chose my clothing carefully, selecting a pair of black cigarette pants from Carrie's closet, a black and white striped V-neck, a long red cardigan, and black bow-tie flats. I curled random sections of my hair, flipped my head upside down and tossed my hair around so it evened out, and stuck a black and silver flower clip on the right side, pulling a section of my hair back and allowing the ringlets to flow loosely around my face. I slipped some silver bangles on my wrist, slid on a chunky onyx ring, and put large silver studs in my ears.

My makeup was simple yet elegant. I highlighted my brow bone with a light mauve with a faint sparkle to it and dusted my lid with a deep maroon. Mascara helped my lashes look effortlessly long and a quick swipe of blush made my cheekbones so sharp they could cut. When I looked in the mirror, I had to grab onto my dresser to steady myself.

Although Carrie and I had always used to play the twin game when we were younger, trying to fool people into thinking we were each other, it had been a long time since anyone hadn't been able to tell us apart. It was always simple, a dramatic, bold eyeliner swoop on my part and subtle, shimmery neutral tones on hers, but it wasn't difficult to tell who was who. Now though, I saw her in myself more than ever.

"Mirror, mirror on the wall, who's the thinnest one of all?" I chided myself softly.

I knew that the answer was Carrie and that it'd take a heck of a lot more dieting to even get to a level where I could be compared to her, but there was nothing like the feeling I'd experienced when I saw her within me.

I grabbed my book bag and slung it over my shoulder, tossing in a water bottle and a banana, figuring my stomach had grown small enough to get used to that kind of sustenance. I opened my door and was surprised to find my mother coming out of her room. We typically didn't cross paths, especially in the morning, and even though I wanted nothing more for her to send me her soft smile and tease me in her lilting voice as she used to most school mornings, I knew that it wouldn't happen. After so long without speaking, I honestly didn't have a clue what to say in front of her, and the awkwardness hung stale in the air.

It wasn't uncommon for her to keep her head down when passing any of us, and especially when forced to go out in public. Today though, she lifted her head before grabbing the doorknob to the bathroom and her face grew so white that it looked almost fluorescent. She gripped the knob so tightly that I thought she was going to rip it off, and her eyes were huge with sorrow, disbelief, and hope.

"Carrie," she croaked almost incomprehensibly, walking towards me and stretching out her fingers to touch me, certain that I had to be a ghost.

Guilt bubbled up at the pit of my stomach, and I felt ashamed for making my mother, who hadn't felt anything in months, feel the hope of seeing her dead daughter again. This time, being mistaken for Carrie was a less than pleasant. It wasn't going to dissuade me from continuing my efforts to become like her, but it was a scene that I'd replay over and over in my head.

"No, Mom," I tried gently, moving to touch her shoulder. "It's just me, Felicia."

She jerked back as though I was going to hit her, and her glazed eyes grew focused in anger. She shot me a look of pure hatred and went into the bathroom, slamming the door behind her so hard that it visibly shook.

My emotions were mixed at the moment. I wanted to feel angry. This woman had given birth to both of us, not just one! I didn't know what it was like to lose someone you had created, a daughter, but I did know what it was like to lose a sister. And we were all mourning, not just her. Where was she to comfort me and Andrew? When she'd given birth, she'd made a vow to care for us all her life, and now we'd suddenly become rejected, almost as though she were sickened just by looking at us because we couldn't bring Carrie back. I know that I sounded terribly whiny, but it wasn't fair. At the same time, I felt guilty, sad that my mother was enduring all of this alone. I was ashamed that I'd given her hope and snatched it away so carelessly.

Chapter 27

As I walked to school, I kicked rocks, ripped flowers from bushes, and spit on the sidewalk. It wasn't exactly a huge stress relief, but it somehow made me feel just a little bit better. Since I'd grown accustomed to not seeing Julian in the hallways, I was sure that he wasn't going to be there and decided to walk through without suspicion or worry. I'd give him a call over the weekend and try to talk him into coming back to school, but I knew that the conversation would be odd.

I fluffed my hair, gave my cheeks a quick pinch for color, and reapplied my lip gloss before strutting down the hallway. Okay, I didn't strut. I wasn't going to change the way I walked, but I suppose there was a little confidence in my step, simply because I know I looked like someone Carrie's friends would want to hang out with. Thanks to my mother, I know I looked like Carrie.

I neared my locker and looked up, curious to see what fabulous outfit Locker Girl was wearing today, certain that she'd have an accessory of worry on her face. Instead, I was stopped in my tracks and had to pick up my jaw from the floor. It took me so long to click my teeth back together that I was reminded of the way my dad used to tease Andrew when he'd watch TV.

"Close your mouth, son. You're letting flies in," he'd chuckle.

My mouth must have been so wide open that enormous mutant flies would have been able to find their way in. Julian, who'd only a few days ago been kissing me in a park, was now leaning over Locker Girl, their faces only inches apart. He smiled down at her, one of his hands casually looped around her waist and the other against his locker, like he was the type of guy who talked to girls like this every day.

She stood there looking nauseatingly cute in fitted black jeans, a button-down plaid shirt, and maroon sneakers. Her hair was pulled back from her face with a feather clip (how dare she!), and I couldn't stop staring at her legs, which seemed thinner than the rest of her body. If there was any part of my body I strived for to be thin, it was most definitely my legs. I tore my eyes away long enough to look back at them.

It was something like a movie scene, a perfect little circle where there wasn't much space between bodies. Next to Julian, she was short and petite and she lifted her head to look up at him, a bright smile on her peach lips. He looked down at her with a similar expression, his once clouded eyes now dreamy, and they looked so picture-perfect that I wanted to rush and break their bond like a game of Red Rover.

It might have been a moment of panic, and deep down I know it was out of pure jealousy, but the next thing I knew, I was pulling a move that was pure Carrie.

"Hey, Josh," I purred sweetly, the words oozing out of my mouth like sweet honey. I sauntered over to him and placed one hand on my hip and tilted my head so that I was at the perfect angle to look up at him, a pose that was classically flirty.

He'd been walking down the hall with some of his friends, wearing a fitted pair of dark rinse jeans and a plain navy shirt under a red and black checkered flannel. His hair was mussed to perfection and he stood tall and solid, looking as though he easily belonged between the pages of a magazine as a model.

"Looking forward to tonight!" I trilled in an unnaturally loud voice, attempting to glance at Julian out of the corner of my eye.

Good. He was looking. Part of me felt sort of lame and a little guilty for using a tactic that I'd have scoffed at months ago, but now, I could see myself easily fitting into Carrie's group. Her friends had never been really nice to me, simply tolerating me when they had to. Josh smiled down at me, and I felt a little flutter of nervousness when I realized that he had always been nice to me. He was different, I decided.

I smirked in Julian's direction and felt a moment of triumph when I saw Locker Girl's expression turn irritated. She'd seemed only indifferent to me before, but now she shot a glare my way that could probably melt ice. Behind Julian and Locker Girl, a sea of students parted to let a group that I highly disliked pass. It was almost disgusting how movie-like the scene was. I wasn't surprised that sunlight came through the windows and bathed the group in a pale golden light. Their hair was bouncy, shiny, and shampoo-commercial ready. I almost laughed out loud at the way they walked, as if they were hoping to be viewed in slow-motion. Their cheerleading uniforms were tight, short, and revealed endless tanned, waxed legs.

Even though I thought their entrance was hilarious, I was also extremely sad. Carrie had been at the center of that line-up, and she'd been able to work it unlike any of them, with a flounce in her step and a sparkle in her eyes that none of them had. She was special.

Their new leader, Jennifer, stopped in the center of the hallway, and her minions nearly tripped over themselves trying to stop in coordination. She was posed with one toe pointed to the left, her hand on her hip, and hungriness in her eyes. She tossed her straight, glossy honey-colored hair over her shoulder and tilted her chin before speaking coolly, directing her gaze towards me.

"Felicia," she stated, with an iciness normally reserved for all of the geeks that were so clearly beneath her.

I waited for a few moments, wondering if she was going to finish her statement. "Yeah?" I asked, a trace of the old, snarky Felicia in the comment.

She smiled for a moment before saying, "I like your shoes. Well, I liked them when they were on Carrie. Sit with us at lunch."

She didn't give me a chance to answer, quickly turning on her heel and (I swear she did this) snapping at the rest of the cheerleaders, who instantly followed her, moving their feet in unison and holding their stances to match hers. It was probably the weirdest moment of my high school career, and I almost laughed at how typical my life had been to a movie lately.

"Cool," Josh said, smiling at me. "Jennifer's great."

I had to stop myself from making a face at his words, instead choosing to smile up at him and echo his words.

"Yeah, she sure is…great," I forced myself to say weakly.

I could almost feel Julian's eyes burning a hole in the back of my head, begging me to turn around so he could laugh at me uproariously, not only for associating with someone who had consistently been mean to us, but for becoming someone I'd only ever made fun of. It wasn't me, and I knew it wasn't, but I was so pleased with everyone's recognition of me as someone they could associate with Carrie that I really didn't care.

Chapter 28

By the time lunch rolled around, I'd touched up my makeup at least three times and debated with myself over what to eat for lunch. If the girls were like Carrie, they'd fix a small bowl from the salad bar consisting of nothing but lettuce, fat-free dressing on the side, and a glass of water. If I didn't eat anything at all, perhaps they'd think I was snubbing them. If Julian could see me now, he'd probably fall over laughing at the effort I was going through to please such a snobby group of people. I shook the thought from my head and walked into the cafeteria, my head held high.

"Felicia!" Jennifer called, her hands in a wave that was as elegant as the Queen's. The entire group looked beautiful, desirable, and completely plastic. My heart sunk a little as I wondered what I was getting myself into. Did I really want a life that was the complete opposite of what I was used to, that stood for everything I was against? Again, I thought of how distant from Carrie my previous life was, and in that moment, nothing mattered but her. I grabbed a saucer-sized plate of lettuce, a couple carrot sticks, and a bottle of water, marching over with all the confidence of a beauty queen.

"Hey!" a chorus of bubbly voices giggled as I sat down. The girls all sat on one side of the table, their petite bodies comfortably spread out to allow room for purses, makeup, miniscule lunch options, and mirrors, but not a single book was in sight. The opposite side of the table almost sagged with the weight that it held. A row of beefy, golden jocks sat together, their trays laden with a variety of sandwiches, pizza, fries, soda, milk, and pudding. All of those carbs and that sugar almost hurt my eyes to look at, and I grabbed my stomach to ignore the hunger pangs that had been hitting me all day.

"Hi," I said awkwardly, doing my best to squeeze in at a table that was already full.

"Over here!" Jennifer cried with all the dazzle of a pageant queen. The spot she was pointing at was the one directly next to the spot that Carrie had always sat. Jennifer now occupied her spot, and she expected me to sit in her old place. I got up to make my way over to that part of the table, and as I did so, I tripped a little. I held my breath, waiting for the peals of laughter that were sure to follow, but they never came. I looked up, surprised to see all of the girls beaming at me. The guys just continued to shovel food into their mouths, and I realized that Jennifer had placed me across from Josh, who sat next to Peter, Carrie's old boyfriend.

"Yo," Peter grunted, barely pausing before he shoved more spoonfuls of mashed potatoes covered in gravy into his mouth.

I politely waved back, somewhat offended that my sister had managed to date this disgusting creature for so long. He'd been in my house so many times that it should have felt somewhat normal to sit next to him, but the big oaf didn't even try to attempt to make conversation, didn't ask how my family was or anything, which made him feel like the stranger I guess he always was.

Josh looked up and smiled at me, but he was deep in conversation with the guy on his right, discussing highlights from last night's football game. I looked to my left and saw a circle of girls engrossed in conversation about the latest brand of mascara and realized that no one was really available for me to actually talk to. I sat there and forked some lettuce into my mouth, wincing at the bitter taste without dressing. I was a Caesar girl through and through, and there was nothing more that I wanted in that moment than a fresh chicken Caesar wrap with lots of parmesan and Romano cheese.

Attempting to distract myself, I threw out a random comment. "So, the lettuce sure is crisp today, huh?"

Everyone stopped eating and stared at me in confusion, and I struggled to fill the awkward silence but came up with nothing. For the rest of the lunch period, I sat dragging lettuce across my plate in silence, wishing I was sitting with Julian.

He sat a few feet away across from Locker Girl. They were both eating chicken sandwiches and had huge brownies on their plates, pastries I recognized as Julian's mother's infamous treats. They were large squares of peanut butter, chocolate, and cheesecake, and I'd never tasted something so delectable. I'd have given anything to be sitting across from him, laughing and gorging myself on brownies instead of sitting here in silence, eating nothing but a couple calories worth of greens. It seemed like the twentieth time I questioned myself that day, but I assured myself that it was worth it for Carrie.

Chapter 29

After school, I raced to the bus and hightailed it out of there. I wanted to look extra special tonight, so I needed to get home for prime primping. After taking a long, hot shower where I scrubbed dead skin cells away with a loofah, used a special scented hair-masque, and luxuriated in a therapeutic body wash, I raced to my room and turned on some music.

My fingers lingered over my old playlist, a selection of 80s music, indie rock, and industrial music, but I forced myself to turn on a catchy pop song that Carrie had always gotten ready to. As I found my body moving to the beat, I realized it wasn't as bad as I thought, but later ended up cringing when I heard the terrible, processed voice. Grizzly, who'd been laying on my bed keeping me company while I got ready, barked in disapproval and leapt off the bed, leaving the room.

"Oh, come on!" I called after him, as though he could understand me. Still, I continued a routine that Carrie had closely followed.

I turned my head upside down and fluffed my hair out, drying it in that position. Apparently it gave your hair more volume, but it just gave me a headache. When I righted myself, I felt dizzy, but I assured myself that it was from having my head upside down. Still, I felt a little nervous, so I chugged some water and ate two cookies from a 90 calorie pack. Instantly, I felt a little better.

My body had been weird the past few weeks. It seemed to be used to receiving such small portions of food, and when I ate too much of anything, even if it was just fruits or vegetables, my stomach felt very full. When I ate, no matter how small the amount of food was, I always seemed to feel satisfied. Of course, this worked for me. I'd been saving my calories all week for tonight. The thought of even touching the greasy, cheesy mess made me sick to my stomach, but I knew that I had to seem normal to Josh. I was tired of the constant headaches, dizzy spells, and hot flashes that had been coming over me, but I was sure I would start eating a little more normally once I reached my goal weight.

I curled the ends of my hair and swept it into a side ponytail, letting wispy tendrils peek out from the sides of my face and fastened the ponytail with a red and turquoise Aztec-style clasp. I highlighted my brow bones with a dusty pink shade, swept a rich brown over my eyelid, and slid a dark maroon color over the crease. I used volumizing mascara that promised to make my lashes appear as though they were false, applying several coats before I was satisfied. When I looked in the mirror, I caught a glimpse of prominent cheekbones that Carrie had always been praised on. My face, though slim, had always been a bit fuller than hers, and my cheekbones didn't stick out nearly as much. Today, however, they looked so nice that I couldn't help but smile.

After allowing myself at least an hour to raid my closet, I decided on a mint green romper dusted with a pale pink and white floral pattern. The romper was belted with a wide, brown crisscrossed belt, and I wore black tights and white oxford shoes, dressed up a bit by the heel. The outfit was sweet enough to be worn by Carrie, but funky enough so that I still looked somewhat like myself. After all of the nagging in the back of my brain this morning, I was afraid that I really was losing myself. The outfit served as a little reminder that I shouldn't get too far gone.

Unfortunately, I still needed her at that moment. I walked carefully to my bed, careful not to rumple my clothes. Sitting primly on the edge, I reached underneath and pulled out the diary, intent on finding an entry that would describe a date with Peter, figuring I'd steal some information on how to act. I just hoped that she didn't describe making out in detail or anything.

I wanted to flip around the diary, but I didn't want to ruin any future entries, knowing I'd need them in the future. Instead, I decided to just randomly open to a page, content with the thought that at least a part of her would be with me tonight.

Things are getting out of control, but there's nothing I can do to stop them anymore. Today, Peter and I went to Haunted Trails for a stress-free day. I was so happy to be able to just let loose for once. This entire week, all I've eaten was a couple broccoli stalks. I tried eating, I really did, but I've honestly completely lost my appetite. After messing around in the arcade and playing mini-golf, Peter wanted to play the batting cages. I wasn't too worried since I was naturally athletic, and if I wasn't any good, I could just giggle and bat my eyelashes out of it. After Peter succeeded in hitting nearly all of the balls, I stepped up to the plate. I lifted the bat and swung as hard as I could. The next thing I knew, I opened my eyes, feeling disoriented. There was pain in my back, legs, and neck, and a crowd of people stood around me, asking if I was alright. I was dizzy, clammy, and remembered nothing. Peter told me that after I swung, I turned white as a ghost and fell to the ground. I didn't eat anything today, but this is the second time something like this has happened. I was forced to eat a stupid funnel cake just to feel better. The calories in that alone were enough to last me the whole week. What a terrible night. I could feel my thighs growing with every bite I took, and when I got home, my stomach looked as though someone attached a beach ball to it. I disgust myself.

I sat there with my hands in my lap, unable to tear my eyes from the page. I remember that day. Carrie had stormed in the house in her little pink dress and the squeal of Peter's tires screeching away (he didn't even walk her to the door—what chivalry!) had filled the whole neighborhood. She hadn't wanted to talk about it, and she'd picked up her diary and furiously scrawled in it before shutting out the lights without my permission and huffing and puffing her way to sleep.

Even though reading her journal entries helped me feel closer to her and inspired me, they also made me feel so sad. Sometimes it was a little too much to believe that she put herself through all of this pain just to look good. Sure, she looked beautiful, but her entries were slowly shedding some light upon the foolishness of her decisions. She was so young! She should have been more worried about school, her date, anything but her calorie count! *Hypocrite*, I thought to myself. *All you worry about is your calorie count.*

109

Chapter 30

My thoughts were interrupted by the doorbell. I looked in the mirror one last time, tucking a loose curl behind my ear before smoothing my romper and slowly walking down the stairs, almost feeling like it was prom night. On my way down, I heard voices and paused for a moment before realizing it was my dad. Curse him! He was hardly ever home, and now he magically showed up to open the door for my date? I gave up preserving my outfit and hair and took the stairs two at a time, skidding to a stop before the doorway.

"What time do you plan on having her home, son?" my dad was asking, trying to sound fatherly but simply sounding awkward.

"I was thinking eleven, sir," Josh grinned, clearly a natural at speaking with parents.

"That sounds about right," my dad said, his voice suddenly becoming gruffer as he tried to appear manlier. I groaned and slapped a hand over my eyes, wanting nothing more than to leave. My prayers were definitely not answered, because I heard a shuffling noise behind me. We all turned around to see my mother. She was dressed in a long white nightgown which hung loosely and looked odd on her tall frame. Combined with her pale pallor, it made her look ghostlike. She shuffled mainly because she couldn't be bothered to lift her feet anymore, but it almost made her look as though she were floating, adding to her eeriness.

My father and I were surprised to see her out of the bedroom, and Josh had a look of shock on his face. Ever the professional, he quickly recovered before saying, "Good evening!"

Though my mom had met him before, a blank look crossed her face before she nodded at him. We all looked at her hands, one of which held a stick of butter and the other which held a fork. The strange combination was a little concerning, but I found myself wondering how the butter got into the fridge.

She shot my dad a look of contempt, a small expression that crossed her face so quickly you could have missed it, but we all saw it. She disappeared back upstairs, and the three of us looked at one another in silence. My life had been filled with awkward silences lately, and I'd had about enough of that. Positive that my parents had greatly embarrassed me, I grabbed Josh's hand, which was surprisingly cool to the touch and large, and hightailed it out the door, not bothering to give my father any details.

The fresh air hit us like the greatest form of relief, and we each drank it in before speaking. "Sorry about that!" I said, trying to sound like it was no big deal.

"Not a problem," Josh said smoothly. "I've always liked your folks."

Yeah, I thought darkly, *you liked them back when they were normal and didn't walk around with weird tans and sticks of butter.* I slapped a smile on my face and we got into the car. The drive to the pizza place was quiet, but he turned on his CD player and the soothing voice of Morrissey filled the car.

"You like the Smiths?" I exclaimed in surprise, reaching over to turn up the volume.

"Hmm," Josh answered unclearly, shooting me a smile and reaching over to place his hand on mine. I was a little put off by his odd answer, but having his hand over mine felt really nice. His hand was large and masculine, and it almost made me feel a little protected. We pulled into Ramoni's and headed inside, the fresh scent of sweet, tangy sauce, buttery crust, and garlic filling the air.

It was crowded, typical for a Friday night. I looked around at the groups of people chatting animatedly in booths, faces that were familiar in appearance but unfamiliar in every other way. We made our way to the center of the parlor, sitting in a booth that was usually reserved for the popular crowd. I started to warn him against sitting there until I realized he was Josh and could do whatever he wanted.

The waitress came almost the second we sat down, and she was so busy flirting with Josh that she seemed to have forgotten our menus. I began to tell her this when Josh cleared his throat and said, "We'll have a large pepperoni and a basket of garlic bread. Oh, and some cheese sticks. And two sodas, please."

I was a little upset that he had ordered without consulting me. It would have been nice if he'd asked what I was interested in having. I was more upset about the amount of food he ordered. Talk about carbohydrates! I smiled weakly as the waitress walked away, and I tried holding a conversation with Josh, but he seemed far away. Every time I thought of something to talk about (and trust me, it wasn't as easy as it sounds), Josh would give me a vague answer and dismiss it. This certainly wasn't the date I'd been looking forward to.

Finally, the waitress came out with a large tray laden with food. She set the steaming dishes in front of us and stood there for a moment, beaming at Josh as though she wanted to watch him take the first bite. I gave her a weird look, and she seemed to take the hint because she frowned and walked away after a moment.

I chose the smallest slice, blotted the grease off the top of the cheese, pulled the pepperoni off, and cut my pizza into the tiniest slivers. By the time I'd forked a couple of them into my mouth, Josh was on his third slice. His plate was heaped with food, and he didn't seem at all embarrassed by the way he was shoveling it in. When I ate with Julian, he was always polite and offered to share with me, and he also knew how to close his mouth when he chewed. But I shouldn't be thinking of him. The door opened, and I half expected him and Locker Girl to walk in, even though it was a place he didn't frequent. Instead it was someone else I didn't want to see.

Chapter 31

Dressed in her usual uniform of sweats, Allison sauntered up to our table with a wide grin on her face. Her baby-haired, stubby dark ponytail flopped around halfheartedly as she walked, and her freckles appeared almost beige under the harsh fluorescent lighting of the restaurant.

"Hey, Josh," she cooed sweetly.

Ever the gentleman, he shot her a winning smile and wiped his lips before balling up his napkin and replying, "How's it going, Al?" (Really? Al?)

"Just fine!" she answered brightly, batting her eyelashes at him but glaring at me the moment he looked down at his pizza. "Josh, we were all wondering...what are you doing out with this loser?"

"Hey, now," Josh said softly. "Felicia isn't a loser. Allison, let's just be cool, alright?"

"Sure!" she responded innocently, a wicked glint in her eye. "Oh," she continued in an unnaturally loud voice, "Freaklicia, I've been meaning to tell you, some Nair should really take care of that hair problem you have! We all noticed it in the locker room, and we're just looking out for you!"

The entire pizza place quieted and all eyes were fixed on me. A few feet away from us, Jennifer was laughing, her wide smile revealing perfectly straight and ultra-white teeth, a clear indicator that she bleached. Her cronies soon followed suit, and only Josh sat there with a perplexed look on his face. My face turned crimson, but all I could do was roll my eyes. She turned around and went to go sit with my new 'friends' and I just snapped.

I began shoveling food into my mouth, not caring that it was cold and tasteless. Four pieces of pizza, two pieces of garlic bread, and six cheese sticks later, I didn't even feel full. Josh was staring at me in awe, but was too polite to say anything. I reached for the last slice of pizza, not caring if I was being rude, and chewed until I felt numb. My stomach finally grew full, the congealed cheese sitting at the bottom of it like an anchor in an ocean, but instead of feeling painful, I simply felt nothing. I was stupid to think that anyone would ever treat me like Carrie just because I dressed like her. I was stupid for going through the whole thing.

"I want to leave," I said to Josh quietly, and he quickly paid the check and came back, grabbing my hand. I was surprised that he was willing to hold hands with me after the whole embarrassing situation, and I heard the buzz of voices grow louder as we walked out the door.

We drove around in silence for a while, and after a few minutes, Josh put his hand over mine again. When we finally pulled up to my house, a soft song was playing in the background and moonlight streamed into the car. The scent of Josh's cologne, woodsy and masculine, filled the air. It was utterly romantic, and surprisingly, I did want him to kiss me. I wanted to know if he was truly different from everyone else, or if his demeanor was just an act.

We sat for a minute, unsure of what to say. Finally, after feeling like nothing was going to happen, I unbuckled my seatbelt and put my hand on the door.

"Wait." Josh reached out and put his hand over my arm, blocking my exit. He pulled me forward so I was facing him and reached out to brush a stray curl behind my ear. He tilted my chin towards him and looked into my eyes for a moment, and the move seemed so premeditated and cheesy that I almost laughed.

Fortunately, the boy was extremely good-looking, so I was able to bear it. His eyes shone with wonder, and his thick hair was as messy as a model's. I wanted to run my fingers through it. I'd never felt this way with a boy before, and I was eager to feel a kiss from someone that I wanted to kiss back. I pushed Julian to the back of my mind again. Why was I thinking about him when I had this gorgeous boy in front of me?

In the next minute, he'd leaned forward and pressed his lips to mine gently. They were soft and warm, and I could faintly taste tomato sauce, which was slightly off-putting, but the kiss was still nice.

In my head, I realized that I'd just described a kiss as "nice." That really wasn't a great adjective. Shouldn't my kisses be amazing, explosive, wonderful? Oh, well. I shut my eyes so tight that my lashes practically brushed my cheek, and I leaned further into him, placing a hand on his chest. It was very broad and well-defined, and since I didn't have much experience in this department, I kind of just let it sit there, which he probably found sort of weird.

We continued kissing, and he started running his hand down my arm and attempting to explore the space above my seatbelt. He ran his finger across my collarbone and I shivered, but I wasn't quite ready to experience anything else at the moment. I began to pull away when he unbuckled his seatbelt and placed both hands around my waist, pulling me forward so I was almost in his lap. His aggressiveness surprised me, and even though it felt good, I didn't want to let things go any further. He crushed his mouth against mine boldly, and he squeezed my shoulder so hard I thought he was going to break the bone.

"Josh!" I exclaimed abruptly, knowing that I needed to put a stop to this.

"Yeah, Carrie?" he panted, moving in to begin kissing me again.

"What!?" I shrieked, the pain so great that it felt as though someone had just socked me in the gut.

"What's wrong?" he asked, genuinely confused. He had just called me Carrie and he hadn't even realized it. This whole time, he was seeking someone else, and I was the person he used along the way.

I could now suddenly feel every bite of food I ate, and I wanted nothing more than to rid my body of it. Josh sat there in a daze, and before I could think, I opened the door and fled from the car, unable to stand there any longer. I heard a weak cry of "Felicia!" before I reached my door, but we both knew that it didn't matter anymore and that there was no use talking about it.

Chapter 32

Despite the incredibly heavy feeling in my stomach, I was suddenly ravenous. I tore into the
kitchen and opened the refrigerator, surprised to see a small collection of white takeout boxes filling the middle compartment. They must have been from one of my father's company dinners.

I opened each one and gazed upon them greedily. The selection was fancy. There was couscous, braised pork loin, beef Wellington, and cheese soufflé. My mouth began drooling as I dumped each item on a plate and stuck it in the microwave. Not able to wait, I ripped open the last box, which held a variety of luscious desserts. I closed my eyes, my hands trembling as I reached chocolate éclairs, chocolate-caramel truffles, triple berry torte, crème brûlée, and mini cheesecake bites. At first, I savored the taste of the delectable treats that had scarcely touched my tongue in recent days. Soon though, my mouth grew numb as the items I was chewing began to hold the consistency of cardboard.

The microwave signaled that the food was ready and I looked down, shocked to see that I had finished the entire box of desserts. I was ashamed, but not ashamed enough. I attacked the plate of hot food with what I thought was relish, but was really just me unable to feel anything at all and confusing my emotions. By the time I'd finished the plate, I felt worse than I had in months. I slumped against the kitchen counter and fell to the floor, remnants of the war zone littered around me. My most recent binge had put the kitchen into an upheaval, and the mess was something I didn't want to touch but knew that no one else would. My father wouldn't notice the missing food. He had brought it home out of courtesy to his colleagues, not because he wanted to eat it.

I was beyond disgusted with myself, and I didn't feel any better. At the time, the motion of pouring food into my mouth seemed to have done a bit to calm the numbness that was slowly spreading over my body, but it was doing nothing now, and if I didn't get the food out soon, I was going to have some more serious problems.

I left the kitchen in disarray and began the retreat to my bedroom. By this point, I was crying so hard that I couldn't even see in front of me. I fell at the foot of the stairs and began crawling up, so weak in mind that I couldn't be bothered to make the decision to put my right foot in front of my left. I don't know how long it took me to get up the stairs, but when I did, I sat in front of my bed and stared into space for a good while. I was angry with myself and angry with Carrie, angry with her friends and angry with my parents.

"Why?" I asked out loud, frustrated beyond belief. "Why did you have to do this to me, Carrie? Why couldn't you have been nicer to me? What happened to us as friends!?" My voice was hysterical at this point, alternating between sobbing and shrieking.

The last time I could remember us really being close was right before we made it to high school. In 8th grade, we were still each other's best friends. We'd wear similar clothing and sometimes even matching clothing in different colors. We were the cute twins, and we ate it all up, using our cuteness as a team, not solo. The day of graduation was one where I'd never felt closer to Carrie.

Night had fallen and we were both in the kitchen, rooting around in the refrigerator for some leftover graduation cake. Carrie cut two slices that were just about identical in size, and she examined them thoroughly before deciding they were equal. We ate in silence, each barefoot and in pajama shorts, our long, tangled hair in matching ponytails. Without makeup on, we looked exactly alike, and we even ate the same way, our motions almost mirrored. We caught each other staring, and we both burst into laughter, loving the twin connection we had.

"I don't want things to change," I said softly, scared of Carrie's response. She had always been the twin who was in charge of all our schemes, the one who made the decisions, and I winced, waiting for her to bossily tell me that I had no choice.

It never came, though. She set down her cake, grabbed me by the shoulders and stared into my eyes, replicas of her own. "Fee, they won't! We're best friends. We're more than best friends; we're twins. No one can ever take that away from us! We have something that no one else could ever have, even if they tried. Remember that!"

I'd smiled in pure delight at that moment, relieved that my sister didn't plan on deserting me. After we'd finished the cake, we grabbed flashlights and snuck out of the house, walking to the little lake a couple miles from our house. The trip was spent telling ridiculously un-scary ghost stories, giggling, and grabbing onto each other's arms when it got too dark. I knew that there could never be another Carrie in my life, and I couldn't wait for us to start high school and begin our reign.

Unfortunately, that reign never included me. Contrary to her promise, things had changed. I soon became less of a friend and more of an annoying sibling. I didn't dress right, speak right, or act right. I know that she still loved me, but her time as queen of the school was consuming, and there was less room for me with the more friends she made.

My face was puffy and covered in tears, streaks of makeup, and as gross as it sounds, dribbles of food. I'd never felt so pathetic in my whole life. It seemed to be a moment of enlightenment for me, though. All I'd wanted the past few months was to be more like Carrie. But since when did that mean sacrificing myself? I decided that things were going to change, starting tomorrow.

Although I wanted to purge more than anything, I forced myself to get into bed and wrapped the covers around the entire bed so I wouldn't think about getting out. Since I'd cried so much, I fell asleep easily and didn't wake until noon. When I was asleep was the best. I didn't have to face reality and I wasn't reminded of all the things that plagued me. Sometimes I wished I could just sleep forever.

Chapter 33

The rest of the weekend flew by uneventfully. My father was barely home and my mother never came out of her room, as usual. I was tempted to go in there and say something to her, to try to make us complete again, but I knew it was no use. Sunday evening, I sat in the living room, lifting small weights while I watched a cooking show. Yes, I did like to torture myself.

The chime of the doorbell was surprising, and I assumed it was probably a Jehovah's witness or something since no one came to see us anymore. I flung the door open, prepared to tell the person that I was highly devoted to God when I got a real shock.

Standing in front of the door looking adorably embarrassed was Josh. He wore black fitted jeans and a forest green hooded sweatshirt, and his hair was mussed perfectly, as usual. I seriously wondered how he did that every day. Did someone purposely mess it up for him before he left his house?

"Hey," he mumbled shyly, looking at the ground and scuffing his feet against the pavement of the walkway. He shoved his hands in his pockets and avoided my eyes, asking, "Do you maybe want to go for a walk? I kind of wanted to talk to you."

I was suspicious, but I was also interested in what he had to say.

"Sure," I replied.

I wore no makeup and had on old sweatpants and an oversized long-sleeved tee shirt that must have been Andrew's, but I made no effort to change or doll myself up. Instead, I slipped on a pair of moccasins that were on the rug and stepped outside into the air, which was cool but not too brisk. The fact that it wasn't cold also made me question Josh's constantly pink cheeks. I sincerely hope he didn't have a professional blush applicator at home.

We walked along in silence for about ten minutes before we reached a small park. He led us to the deserted playground, and we each sat on a swing and started pumping our legs, needing to let out energy that words weren't sufficient for just yet. After swinging for a few minutes, he finally spoke, slowly at first, but quickly picking up the pace as he became more passionate.

"Felicia, I want to apologize. I can understand how much you must have hated me after I called you Carrie, and believe me, I hated me too. I know you probably think that I used you, but I really didn't. And I know you were probably mad at me for not sticking up for you at Ramoni's; I spent a while hating myself for that too. But even though there's no excuse behind any of my actions, maybe if I tried to clarify some things, you could look at it differently.

Even though the time I "dated" your sister was brief, and we were really young, there was something about her that I could never let go of. By the time high school rolled around, Peter was the biggest, the strongest, the coolest, and I was only second best. I admit that there were some times I probably didn't treat Carrie so well because I was trying too hard to fit in and be one of the guys, which apparently meant that I had to be a jerk. She was moving up the ladder too, so it was no wonder that she and Peter dated. They were practically meant for each other.

Even while they were dating, I still felt like I was in love with her, as silly as it sounds. I know that I was extremely young and probably didn't know what love was, but I know it wasn't what she and Peter had. He never had much to say about her except typical guy comments like, "She's hot," or other stupid things. She seemed more like an accessory to him than a girlfriend, someone he could parade around to complete the perfect jock/cheerleader expectation. When I saw her, I thought she was beautiful.

I wanted to hold her hand and tell her how beautiful she was. I pictured us walking in time to a music video. It was just ridiculous. I loved her laugh, the things she said, the fact that she was so much more beneath that cheerleader façade. She was smart. She was real. I know that you know what I'm talking about. Jennifer and Allison are perfect examples of what Carrie wasn't. She was glossy outside, but she was more perfect inside."

By this point, I was crying. I think that Josh was struggling not to, and his words tumble out quickly, but every single one is important.

"When she died, I was beyond crushed. I know it's nothing compared to what you or your family felt, but I felt like I was losing the one person I wanted to keep knowing for years and years. I didn't feel like that about anyone else at school. I had no one to talk to about it. Peter kept his thoughts to himself and all the girls just cried without really talking about it. As selfish as this is for me to say to you, no one was there for me to talk to.

I need you to know that it wasn't my intention to use you or make you feel like you were being used. Honestly, I've always liked you a lot! But it had been months since I'd seen or spoken to you, and when I saw you in that hallway, it almost wasn't you. I just saw Carrie."

My heart sank as he said the words, which struck me as odd. This is what I wanted, wasn't it? First my mom and now Josh. I wasn't as good as Carrie. I was just her substitution. It had been my goal, but somehow, it didn't feel like the euphoria I expected to feel. When I was younger, my mom had always warned me of being careful of what I wished for. Here was all the proof I needed.

His face was red, not only from the cold but from the frustration of telling me something he'd held in for so long and from the embarrassment of admitting something he found faulty in himself. I couldn't speak yet, and I'd stopped swinging a long time ago, sitting silently and gripping the metal chains harder as he continued to speak.

"I wasn't trying to substitute her with you, but you just looked so beautiful and full of life, and I missed her so much that I wasn't thinking. I mean, you even sounded like her on the phone. It was like, for one second, I had her back in my life, and I felt like I was on top of the world. I mean, there was some nagging going on in the back of my head that something about this wasn't quite right, but it just felt for a moment like I had my old life back again.

There's nothing that I can really say or do to make this better, but I really just wanted to apologize face-to-face. I hope you know how much I really cared about your sister..." he finished lamely.

I sat there silently for a moment, folding my hands over and over and licking my lips in an almost obsessive manner before I was able to speak. It was painful to hear Josh's words, but there was also a sense of relief there.

While Josh was a beautiful boy, I didn't laugh with him. I wasn't able to sit there in silence and feel comfortable. And I couldn't imagine having him in my life every day. I pushed the thought of Julian out of my mind and thought about the current moment. I realized that it was going to be okay, and even though I felt miserable, another part of me was touched that he'd cared enough to come talk to me about all of it.

"Josh," I began slowly, "It's okay. We can be...friends?"

"Friends!" he echoed, relief evident in his voice. We stayed at the park for at least another hour, occasionally talking. Mostly, we sat on the swings and each stared into the distance, finally able to feel comfortable enough to sit pensively without it feeling too awkward.

By the time it started getting dark out, we each mustered smiles and walked together to my house. Josh offered me his sweater when it got a little windy, which was sweet, but we both knew that being close was no longer an option. When we got to my door, I promised him that I would continue to talk to him. I stood in the living room and watched him walk down the street, his tall figure finally retreating into the darkness.

Chapter 34

After Josh left, I pulled the filmy curtains shut and glanced down at my hands, slightly surprised to find dirt there. I knew things hadn't been cleaned in a long time, but I didn't know it was this bad. I don't know if I felt like I had to clean my mind of what had just happened or I just needed something to do, but I went down to the basement and got some supplies.

Armed with bleach, paper towels, spray cleaners, vacuum powder, dust rags, wood cleaners, and a broom and mop, I set to work. About two hours later, the downstairs area looked far better than it had, but was nothing compared to what my mother ever did.

On Saturday mornings, while we were busy eating donuts, sunbathing, or getting ready to go out, my mother would be dressed in a tee-shirt and shorts, happily scrubbing every inch of the house. She'd sing and whistle while she worked, and my dad sometimes called her "Cleany," the 8th dwarf.

I really wonder what happened to her. I know that Carrie was her child, and nothing can ever replace a child or soothe the loss of a child. Trust me, I was finding that out on my own. But I'd never thought things would get to the point where a woman who was once the brightest, most cheerful woman any of us could know would lock herself in her room every day and let herself waste away.

On Friday nights, she and my father would have date nights. Carrie and I loved watching her get ready, a magical process that seemed to fascinate us. She would sit in front of her vanity mirror, a large round piece of glass with bright bulbs that circled it, a mirror that

Carrie and I often would sit in front of after sneaking in her room and pose for hours.

My mother would sift through all of her dresses, silky fabrics of peach, lilac, and cerulean colors blending together. I remember standing in the doorway with Carrie and watching her run a round brush through her thick hair and carefully fasten two sparkling earrings to her ears. A flick of mascara and a brush of blush and she would be done, her face radiant even without makeup. She'd turn around and smile a huge smile that exposed nearly all of her straight, dazzling teeth and she'd ask, "What do you girls think? Pretty enough to go out with Daddy?"

My dad would dance into the room and lift her to her feet, sweeping her around the floor for a minute before lowering her into a dramatic movie-kiss pose and twirling her back upwards, exclaiming, "I'm not worthy! I'm not worthy!"

"Oh, Adrian!" my mother would giggle. My father was the only person who could make her actually giggle. It was these sweet moments that we loved seeing. We'd roll our eyes and I'd stick my finger above my tongue and pretend to gag while Carrie would cross her eyes and pretend to choke herself. It was silly, but it was also a ritual I'd give anything to relive.

After putting everything away and realizing that nobody was going to come down and tell me how nice it looked and comment on how nice it was for me to do it without even being asked, I trudged upstairs to my bedroom and quietly got ready for bed. I hadn't eaten anything today and didn't want to after that horrible binge I had. I didn't know how many calories it'd all come out to, but it would probably be more than I'd eaten in weeks. I was surprised at how well I'd been doing not eating, but I was really distracted with everything else going on.

I stood up and walked to the mirror, lifting my shirt up to examine my stomach. It looked flatter than it had before, but I frowned at the small layer of fat that seemed to curl over my waistband. My legs looked the same, which bothered me immensely. No matter what I did, they never seemed to change. If only they could be as thin as Locker Girl's. I sighed, admonishing myself for not taking care of that binge when I had the chance. I started to do some leg kicks, but realized I was simply too exhausted. Having had enough of my melancholy mood, I climbed into bed without bothering to finish my routine and crept into a silent, dreamless sleep.

Chapter 35

I woke up late the next morning. There was no time for the Carrie routine, and part of me wasn't even sure if I wanted to continue it. Not really bothering to look good for anyone, I slipped on a pair of dark jeans, teal sneakers, and a gray windbreaker. I jammed a gray knit cap on my head and was down the stairs. I stopped in the kitchen (which was now clean!) and thought about grabbing a banana, which didn't have too many calories in it, but felt too tired to eat. Shrugging, I tossed the banana back in the bowl and was out the door. They were nearly black anyway.

When I got to school, I kept my head down and walked quickly to my locker, unwilling to meet the eyes of any students around me, innocent or not. I managed to get through most of the day without having to deal with anyone, spending my lunch period in the library. I was sitting in the corner and reading a fashion magazine, scrutinizing the bodies of each and every model featured. They all seemed too perfect, possessing no stretch marks, wrinkles, or an ounce of fat. They were beyond beautiful, and I felt hopeless in thinking I'd ever look like that. On a whim, I ripped out a few of the pictures for inspiration and stuffed them in my pocket stealthily before resuming my reading.

"Excuse me," the cranky old librarian asked in a foghorn voice. She peered over her glasses which were secured to her face in an actual chain and demanded that I present my lunch pass to her.

"I, um, forgot it?" I said lamely, hoping she'd be happy I was reading and just let it go.

She wasn't. She yanked me up from the chair and sent me over to one of the security guards, who promptly escorted me to the cafeteria. By this point, there was no doubt in my mind that my life had become a movie. The entire room didn't fall silent, but it was a lot quieter after I'd entered. Every person at my sister's table sat with their eyes fixed on me. Josh was the only person who continued to eat, and I could see him doing what he could to try to get everyone's attention, but no one was falling for it. This was much juicier.

I began walking towards the back of the cafeteria when I heard Jennifer call my name. I froze for a moment but continued walking, reminding myself that every person at that table had been in uproarious laughter at Ramoni's. Despite my obvious walking away from the table, my name continued to be called. Jennifer did not like that she wasn't getting a response, and I could see that this wasn't going anywhere pretty.

She'd never liked being second-best to Carrie. She was always a little more selfish, a little more demanding, and a lot meaner. Although she was one of Carrie's good friends, I'd always got the impression that she truly didn't like anyone, so I wasn't surprised that she wanted to make my life miserable now. I found it almost pathetic that they would attack the twin sister of their deceased friend, and that thought made me turn around.

I pivoted expertly and marched over to the table, my chin in the air and my eyes fixed on Jennifer. Carrie's spot was filled, but my eyes were glued to the seat next to her, where Allison sat. I nearly laughed out loud. What was this, a movie where I was being confronted by the mafia and its assassins? Allison had never been a source of teasing for Jennifer and her friends, but they didn't hang out together either. I knew that this didn't look good.

Looking to the left, I saw Julian staring at me, a concerned look on his face. He sat with Locker Girl, of course, and an untouched tray sat in front of him. That was strange. Julian was thin, but he was always hungry, and he'd usually eat whatever I didn't finish. I felt a twinge of worry, but I reminded myself that I didn't need to be concerned anymore. Locker Girl could handle it.

By the time I reached the table (after walking to my head's soundtrack of Joe Esposito's "You're the Best," from *Karate Kid*), I was greeted by a creepy sight. Each of the cheerleaders sat with their hands folded and their heads cocked to the left side, a small smile on each of their faces. This was Stepford eerie.

"What's up?" I asked casually, yawning as though I were bored even though I could feel myself shaking. One thing I knew from Carrie is that acting like you didn't care in front of the cheerleaders was bound to tick them off. There was nothing they hated more than not having someone's full attention, and I was ready for the challenge.

"Allison has brought you a present," Jennifer said sweetly, gesturing to the brunette devil sitting beside her.

Allison reached into her backpack and pulled out a large bottle of Nair, a box of waxing strips, and a bag of razors, holding them up high so the entire cafeteria could see them.

"This will surely take care of your problem!" she said wickedly, tossing them in my direction even though she knew I wouldn't catch them.

I could do nothing but roll my eyes. Honestly, I was past being embarrassed at this stage. No one really liked me anyway, and it's not like I cared about them before. Still, I could feel tears forming in the corner of my eyes as I turned away. I wanted to do one thing for Carrie, one thing to let her know how much she meant to me, and I couldn't even do that right. I felt like a failure. I couldn't lose weight, I couldn't be popular, and I couldn't live up to my sister's legacy to make her happy.

I'd taken only a step when my head started to feel heavy. I began blinking furiously, unable to stop the spread of black fuzziness before my eyes. I reached out and grabbed the closest thing to me, which just so happened to be Jennifer. I'd almost fallen, but after a moment, my vision returned and I was able to stand upright.

"Ew!" she shrieked, jerking away from me. "What are you like, in love with me or something?" she whined, receiving applause and laughter from her faithful minions, Allison included.

Josh shot me a look of sympathy but I averted my eyes. He almost looked as though he were contemplating whether he should say something, but apparently my "friend" decided against it, returning to his food. I felt weak and off-balance, but I just wanted to get out of there.

I managed to catch Julian's eyes again before I left, and his gaze was intense, part angry and part worried. He looked as though he wanted to rush over to me, and I could see him move his chair back, but Locker Girl's hand quickly trapped his arm, and he settled back in his chair. Part of me was furious with him for not chasing after me, but what did I expect? I'm the one who turned him away. I'm the one who created my own loneliness.

Chapter 36

The day was excruciatingly long, and I felt a huge sense of relief when the last bell rang. I was walking to my locker when Martha, a girl in my math class who I used to talk to last year tapped me on the shoulder. She was a really nice girl and I'd almost become friends with her before everything changed.

"Hi," I said, summoning a weak smile.

"Hi, Felicia," she said shyly, pushing her glasses up her nose. She was of average weight and height and had shiny black hair that she always wore in a ponytail. Jennifer's crowd had dubbed her a nerd, but she was smarter and a heck of a lot funnier and more interesting than any of them.

"Um, don't get mad at me for saying this," she said quickly, "but I've noticed that you've lost a lot of weight lately and I was just wondering if you were doing okay? I mean, I'm not trying to get into your business at all, but in the last few months, all your clothes just kind of hang off of you. And your cheekbones look sort of hollow, and you always look pretty tired."

Martha was normally a very quiet girl, and I don't think I'd ever heard her say that much at one time before. She was staring at me with an anxious look in her warm brown eyes, afraid that she'd offended me but eager for me to assure her that all was well and that I was fine.

"Martha, it's nice of you to ask, but I have no idea what you're talking about," I replied. It came out more curtly than I'd intended it to, and she looked taken aback.

"I-I'm sorry," she stuttered quietly, her eyes flashing stormy with hurt. "I just…I'm not the only one who's noticed, and I just wanted to see…"

"See what?" I cut her off. "You think it's funny to make fun of me because I'm not as thin as everyone else? Is it okay to make fun of chubby people now or something?"

I was yelling at her now, and I didn't know why, nor did I know exactly what I was saying, but I know it was what I felt inside. A flashback of the day at the creak with Carrie went through my mind, but I pushed it away.

"What?" she gasped, unable to comprehend. "Chubby? Is that a joke? I can see all your bones! You don't even look pretty anymore," she spat, her face growing red with anger.

I'd never seen this side of her before, and it wasn't something that I liked, and I'm sure she didn't like my attitude either.

Her face quickly changed to sorrow, and she stopped, pausing before saying, "I didn't mean that, Felicia. I just…you should know that you don't look the same anymore, and I'm just not sure it's in the best interest of your health."

"Thanks," I said noncommittally, unable to look her in the eye. I walked away but could feel her eyes on my back, and I felt terrible that I'd treated her that way.

On my way home, all I could think about was our conversation. It kind of reminded me of some of the things everyone was saying to Carrie. No matter what they said, she'd refuse to believe them. But we all saw her body changing with our own eyes. This wasn't the same, though, I assured myself. Not nearly the same.

Chapter 37

After unsuccessfully trying to finish my homework, I decided to pamper myself a bit. Since it wasn't very warm outside, I hadn't shaved my legs lately. I guess that's what Allison and Jennifer were talking about. Big deal. My leg hair wasn't that dark anyway, and gym class wasn't coed, so I didn't see what the problem was. That school was so superficial.

I walked to the bathroom and undressed, standing beneath the brightest lights in the house. They were incredibly annoying when going to the bathroom in the middle of the night, as your eyes had to force themselves to adjust. However, they really came in handy when putting on makeup or plucking eyebrows. I turned towards the mirror, ready to pinch and poke the flesh that settled heavily on my body. Instead, I let out a soft cry, shocked at what I saw instead.

A fine downy hair covered my shoulders and arms. I turned around and saw it scattered across my back, and it even appeared to be lightly poking out on my cheeks. My heart started pounding irregularly, and I got as close to the mirror as I possibly could without actually touching it. What in the world was this? I felt like some kind of animal, and never had I felt my hope more lost than at that moment.

Panicking, I fled out of the bathroom without bothering to put my clothes on and raced into my bedroom, flipping open my laptop and barely waiting for it to start up before doing a quick Internet search for body hair. After clicking through some truly terrible photos of men covered in hair, hair removal ads, and more armpit hair pictures than I'd ever wanted to see in my life, I found a link that looked worthy of clicking on. The pictures featured on the site were of girls who had conditions very similar to mine.

"Just tell me what it is!" I said, frustrated, making several clicks before I found a definition. Lanugo? The site defined it as a soft hair that grew over the body as a protective mechanism to keep the body warm due to starvation or malnutrition.

"Impossible," I scoffed, shutting my laptop closed. Still, something was nagging at me. The photos I'd seen looked just like what I'd viewed in the mirror.

"I'm not starving!" I said out loud to no one. It had only been a few months since my diet plan began. I know I cut back on eating kind of abruptly, but it couldn't be something so serious. Still, just to be on the safe side, maybe I'd start eating a little more. But not until tomorrow.

Chapter 38

The next day, I ate an old apple before I left for school. It was soft and kind of flavorless, so it wasn't the best thing I'd ever tasted, but it was something. I also packed a whole grain muffin and some carrot sticks. I had to force myself to eat those, and I wanted to gag and I had no idea why. I didn't seem to have too much trouble polishing off that pizza or desserts.

By lunchtime, I strode into the cafeteria confidently, ignoring the evil table. I walked straight into the line, determined to buy something. When I reached the counter, I contemplated between a small cup of green beans or a plate of tofu and rice. I heard someone's throat clear behind me and realized Martha was standing there. I'll show her, I thought.

I set the green beans down and reached for a thick, gravy-laden roast beef sandwich that came with fries. The smell of it made me feel sick, but I paid for it anyway. Her eyes stayed on me as I walked over to an empty table near the doors. I took a bite, an overpowering wave of nausea coming over me. I squeezed my eyes but continued to eat, stuffing the bread into my mouth and forcing myself to swallow. An old favorite of mine, it now tasted absolutely terrible. I could feel a heaviness settling in my stomach, and it was all I could do to keep myself from keeling over and grabbing it. By the time I'd stuffed the last fry in my mouth, I felt even worse than I had after the binge. This was, in a sense, a binge since I hadn't eaten anything that bad or in that quantity in so long.

I flashed a smile at Martha, who was looking at me curiously. Then

I quickly got up and raced out of the cafeteria, needing to be anywhere but there. The fullness in my stomach made me feel incredibly disgusting, and I wanted to get rid of it as soon as possible. No! It was important that I kept myself semi-healthy. I'd managed to keep myself from purging last time; I could do it again this time.

But I couldn't. I looked around the empty hallway and ducked into the staff-only one-person bathroom. Opening my mouth, I stuck my finger as far back into my throat as I could, feeling myself start to gag. Tears welled up in my eyes and the familiar raw, burning feeling came to my throat, one that wasn't supposed to feel good but was something I welcomed.

My lunch came up in chunks. I'd eaten so fast that I'd barely chewed my food, and I was lucky that none of it got lodged in my throat and choked me. When it was over, I grabbed a paper towel and wiped the sweat off my forehead. The same powerful feeling I felt every time came over me, and I just couldn't regret it. Most people gained weight because they couldn't undo what they ate, but I could, and I wasn't going to stop just so some girl I barely talked to could be satisfied.

After waiting in the bathroom for a few minutes, I opened the door and slowly stepped outside, making sure no one saw me. I thought I was in the clear until I saw Martha across the hall, standing there with her arms folded and looking at me accusingly.

"What are you like, stalking me?" I blurted, instantly regretting how much I sounded like Jennifer.

"No," she said snippily, clear hurt in her eyes. "What did you do in there?"

"Excuse me?" I said in disbelief. "Last I checked, there was only one use for bathrooms. That's really not something you should be interested in anyway. That's kind of odd."

She shook her head and began walking away, then paused, as though she were reflecting upon something. She turned back around and held a warning finger in the air, looking me straight in the eyes and said, "You might think that you're fooling everyone, but if you keep it up, I'm not going to hold back. In your best interest...I'll tell."

I panicked inside but feigned indifference. "What are you even talking about? You're good at math -- shouldn't you know how to use reasoning and deduction? Guess not," I replied, walking away quickly, my body shaking.

As I walked home, I wondered what Martha could possibly see that made her so judgmental. Yes, my goal was to lose weight, and yes, I'm sure I lost a little, but there was absolutely no way that I lost enough for her to freak out over. She was probably jealous, I decided. Yes, jealous that so many new people were paying me attention and I had less time for her. Right, Felicia. Because you have so many friends.

Chapter 39

I was halfway to my house when my phone began ringing. It was a number I didn't recognize, and I answered in dread, praying it wasn't Jennifer and her stupid friends prank-calling me.

"Hello?" I asked, somewhat defensively.

"Hi!" the voice on the other end chirped, full of cheer. "We're just calling to remind you that you have a dentist appointment today at 4:00!"

Ugh. I'd forgotten about my six-month checkup, and the dentist was in the other direction. I reluctantly turned around but felt a little better when I realized the calories I'd burn would double. It took me a short amount of time to get there since I walked very fast. I sneered at the giant plastic waving tooth that greeted patients as they entered the office's corridor. When I was a child, I thought it was adorable, but now it just looked silly.

"Hi, Felicia!" the same gleeful voice sang, beckoning me to enter the back. The hygienist did the usual: flossed my teeth, cleaned them, and gave them a fluoride treatment. She kept asking me questions even though it was clearly impossible to answer them, and when she finished, she told me to wait for the doctor to check my teeth.

I probably waited for about ten minutes until he entered. He was tall and somewhat menacing, a looming figure in white. He had thick dark hair sprinkled with gray and a huge, white smile. He was brisk and got right to the point, turning his flashlight-headband contraption on and peering into my mouth.

"Mmm," he said, with a slight frown. I was a little worried. Usually, he looked at my teeth, told me they looked great, and I was on my way. After looking for a little while longer, he sat back and removed his gloves.

"Felicia," he began gravely, "I'm noticing some tooth decay and gum damage. Have you been taking care of your teeth?"

"Of course!" I squeaked, worry in my voice.

"I'm going to be straight with you, Felicia. There is hardly any enamel left to your teeth. A couple in the back are almost crumbling, and if we don't take care of it, they can fall out."

"Why?" I gasped. He nodded at the hygienist, who grabbed my files and left the room, shutting the door behind her.

"Typically, we see this pattern of tooth decay in patients who excessively induce vomiting. Does this apply to you?" he asked softly, staring me directly in the eye.

"No!" I answered defensively.

He twisted his lips, giving his face a perplexed expression. "Felicia, I'm going to give you a pamphlet on some of the dangers that can arise from improper care. I'm also going to give you a medicated mouthwash to try to strengthen your enamel. However, it does stain your teeth. If we don't improve, we're going to be facing some problems."

We? I thought bitterly. *I didn't realize we were in this together.* I kept myself from rolling my eyes and nodded stiffly, removing the pink paper sheet that was tied around my neck to catch drool.

Walking home, I felt betrayed for some reason. In the past few months, all I'd done was try my hardest to live the life Carrie couldn't live for her. And all I had to show for it was body hair and rotten teeth. By the time I got to my doorstep, I had to nearly drag myself inside, and my shoulders were so low that I stood at almost half a foot shorter than my normal height. All I wanted to do was crumple to the ground.

Chapter 40

I decided to ignore my homework, even though I'd actually been doing a much better job of completing it in the last few months since it was a distraction from eating. Instead, I plopped down on the couch, clean and fresh-scented from my recent therapeutic cleaning session. I grabbed an old throw blanket that Carrie, Andrew, and I always used to fight over and threw it over my legs, leaning back to find a comfortable position. I started watching a children's channel, which was somewhat comforting.

The next thing I knew, I felt the blanket slide up over my shoulders. A large, cool hand pressed down upon my forehead, and I heard the gentle click of the television being shut off. I shot up, somewhat afraid to hear the silence.

"Hey, kiddo," my dad said softly, kneeling next to me with a small smile on his face. Just for a minute, I was a kid again. I had fallen asleep on the couch and my dad was here to throw me over his shoulder and carry me up to my bed, and even though he knew I was just pretending to be asleep, he did it anyway, no matter how old I got.

His eyes twinkled slightly, and they were so familiar that I couldn't help but feel somewhat ashamed that I thought he was messing around on my mother. Still, there were too many things that were unexplained. He made a move like he was going to grab me, and it almost made me laugh, knowing that he didn't actually plan on carrying a seventeen-year-old upstairs.

"I'm worried about you. You look tired. You look older. You look... not yourself."

"Gee, thanks, Dad," I said sarcastically. "What a great accusation to wake up to." I yawned, holding my hand up to cover my mouth.

"What is this?" he nearly yelled, grabbing my arm to examine it. My skin, paler than usual, was dotted with several dark bruises in different shapes and sizes, ranging in color from deep purple to fluorescent yellow.

"I don't know," I breathed, startled myself. Tears started forming in my eyes, and the salty drops spilled over my cheeks in a flow that was almost unstoppable. What was happening to me? I tried to get up to get away when I realized I couldn't. My body was somehow frozen.

"Dad!" I cried, but my voice just came out mumbled. It was almost like sleep paralysis. I tried desperately to move, but my muscles wouldn't give in. It lasted for about another thirty seconds, and I was in complete panic before I was able to move again.

"Felicia! What is going on?" my dad screamed, fear in his voice. "You can't...you can't turn into your sister on me!" he choked out, putting his head into his hands.

All expression left my face, and I could only look at him for a moment, not fully registering what he was saying. His shoulders shook lightly, and he didn't remove his hands from his face. I left him in peace, quietly leaving the room, my legs feeling tight and cramped, my body afraid that it was going to spasm again.

Once I got to my room, I needed Carrie more than ever. How was I going to fix all this? She'd never mentioned losing weight being this hard or this scary. I dropped to my knees and crawled over to my bed, afraid to use my muscles any more than I had to. Her journal in hand, I sent her a silent note that there'd be some kind of advice in there.

I'm sick to my stomach right now. Or I would be, if there was anything in there. My hair is my best feature. It's long, thick, and extremely healthy looking. After my morning shower, I was in the process of brushing my hair when I realized the brush wasn't really working anymore. I held it out to clean it and was shocked at the huge ball of hair that chose to make the brush its new residence. I reached behind my head to run a hand through my hair and came out with one clump, and then another, and another. My skin is always so dry that no moisturizer can help its constant cracking. What a monster I'd become.

All I wanted was to feel prettier but instead I'm uglier than ever. I still find it hard to understand why this is happening. No matter how little I eat, I'll never look the way I want to. It's been drilled into my head. Still, there's no stopping it. Even if I tried, there's no stopping it.

What was Carrie talking about? Stopping what? And she'd been losing her hair? Again, I felt more guilty than imaginable after realizing that there were a lot of things I really didn't know about my sister before she'd died. I was restless and frustrated, so I went back downstairs to see if I could fall asleep by the television again.

My dad was in my spot, his head rested on the foot of the couch and his mouth open, his signature sleeping pose. It almost made me smile, and I reached over to tug the blanket over his chest when my hands brushed a metal, jagged object. My dad's key ring! My entire body started trembling, both in excitement and fear. I wasn't sure what I'd find waiting for me at the bottom of that file cabinet, but I was almost certain it would explain my dad's strange behavior.

I gently began working the key ring through his pants loop, and was almost finished when he started to move. No! He groaned and mumbled something in his sleep before turning away from me, rolling over onto the side his keys were hanging. I breathed in deeply and blew air out between my teeth, trying my best to remain calm. This wasn't over, I told myself. I would find out what was in that cabinet, even if it killed me.

Chapter 41

As I tossed and turned in bed that night, my mind raced through the day's events. It was clear that something was consuming me, but I wasn't sure how it all seemed to come together at one time, seemingly out of nowhere. I was restless, even after doing 5 sets of 100 crunches.

For the past few months, nearly every night ended with me exercising. I'd started walking whenever I could, avoiding the bus for the most part. Waking up was no longer a problem, because I was eager to start the day with some sort of exercise. Other than that fateful day with Josh, my beverage choices were limited to water, natural tea, or 100% juice, a rare treat. Fast food had been completely eliminated from my diet, and after overhearing a classmate brag about her newfound vegan lifestyle, I'd started to cut most meats and dairy.

In an average day, I'd say I'd eat some sort of fruit for breakfast, a salad without dressing for lunch, and a vegetable or tofu for dinner. Each meal was accompanied by a diet pill, and although I'm not sure they helped with losing weight, they did seem to curb hunger. There was no such thing as 'snacks' in my diet, and if I ever felt faint during the day, I'd chug a bottle of water until my stomach felt full. If I was really woozy, I'd buy a 100 calorie pack from the vending machine, eat 5-10 pieces, and throw the rest away. My routine had become one I looked forward to. Whenever I made it through the day on as little as six bottles of water and a small plate of zucchini, squash, and eggplant, I felt triumphant.

Martha's words seemed to resonate within me that night. She thought I looked skinnier, Julian had mentioned I looked thinner, my mom had mistaken me for Carrie, and my dad almost started crying about something or other. Could it really be possible? Had I in fact lost some weight?

Throughout my months of dieting, I'd never actually weighed myself out of fear that I wouldn't be able to live up to Carrie. While we weren't super tall, we were around an average height, taller than most of the girls in our grade. I'd read somewhere that a healthy weight for being about 5'5-5'6 was between 125 and 135. I know Carrie was far below that, and I couldn't imagine I was anywhere near what she was. After tonight though, I needed to know.

I got up and started rooting around the closet. There was no way she'd have dieted so exceptionally without weighing herself once in a while. My search proved to be futile. I tapped my fingers against the side of the closet, thinking for a minute before racing over to her hamper. Since both of us had an almost irregular amount of clothes in our wardrobe, our mom had long given up on us sharing a hamper, and had bought two cute ones that almost looked like room decorations. Since they went together, I hadn't ever removed hers, but I did remember her hiding things at the very bottom. A report card, a letter from Peter, a pack of cigarettes, anything she didn't want our parents to see.

I walked over and pushed on it. Heavy, just as I'd suspected. All that was in the hamper was a sheet and an old sweater of mine. I knew she just used those items to make it look full. At the bottom, though, was gold. I reached down and felt my hands scrape against cool metal and plastic. I lifted it out and gazed at it, pleasantly surprised by the digital model.

I brought it to the bathroom, locking the door behind me. Gazing into the mirror, I saw someone who resembled Carrie, but not closely enough. My cheekbones didn't seem as hollow as hers had been, my clavicles weren't as prominent, and I didn't have that tiny shoulder bone that stuck out like hers did. Still, I had to admit that I was visibly thinner, although clearly not thin enough. Underneath my eyes were bags that were bluish in color, puffy as though I'd been crying, which I suppose I had. I was still confused about what was going on in my body, but the pale sight of me, bonier than I'd been before, slightly cheered me.

I set Carrie's scale down, took a deep breath, and stepped onto it. My eyes were closed for almost a minute, and I was slightly terrified to look down. The last time I'd been on a scale, it had been at a doctor's office, where I'd weighed around 126 pounds, which the doctor proclaimed had been perfect. Carrie, I remember, had given me a look of disgust, quickly covered by a weak smile. I hadn't missed it though, and I wished she could see me now.

Finally, I was brave enough to look down. The digital numbers blinked up at me. 98. My stomach turned. Ninety-eight? This couldn't be right. I had dreamed about being under 100 pounds, but there was absolutely no possible way that I'd lost nearly thirty pounds in just a few months. Yes, my diet seemed a bit extreme, and I was taking pills and exercising almost compulsively, but what about my binges? Sure, I'd purged for some of them, but not all of them.

The scale was wrong, I decided simply. It'd been sitting at the bottom of Carrie's hamper for months. The thing was probably broken or needed new batteries. I might have looked a little thinner, but it definitely wasn't that thin. 98 would be a dream come true. I felt disgusted with myself and marched back to my room, throwing the scale in the garbage can, where it landed with a loud bang. The mirror was the only object that could determine my weight.

Chapter 42

By morning, I realized that I'd only slept about an hour. I had absolutely no energy, having been awake all night staring at the ceiling and debating whether or not I should try to shave the weird hairs that were beginning to cover my body. Still, I woke up and did some jumping jacks, lunges, and push-ups. I skipped breakfast, deciding to buy coffee on the way to school. I hated the taste, but I needed to wake up, and there was no point in wasting calories on fruit when I knew that the coffee was double what I should have.

My hair was tangled and unwashed, but I braided it. Unwilling to look in the mirror, I chose the baggiest sweatshirt I could find and paired it with an oversized pair of jogging pants. If I didn't think my body was worthy of looking at, I'm sure no one else did either. The pants slipped down a couple times, but I'm sure that was just from them being old and worn-out. Deciding that I needed to change my tactics after last night's ordeal, I took two diet pills, hoping it might speed my metabolism along.

I'm sure I sound crazy, since just a day or two ago I vowed to eat better after noticing the hair, but it was impossible for me to feel anywhere near good about myself after the scale incident. I know Carrie went under 100, but she was still beautiful. Long and graceful, like a swan. I wasn't long or lean and everyone knows I was far from graceful. I wanted so badly to be at the level she was at, but I was certain I had a long way to go. I reached school a bit early, feeling like a college student in my sweats and toting a coffee. I was glad that I didn't have to see too many people wandering the hallway, especially

Martha. Who knows what she'd say today?

I made it to my first class in one piece, without being the target of anyone. It was an Honors class, so I didn't have to worry about Jennifer or any of her mindless friends being in there. Julian was in the second section, so I was feeling pretty free. I could sit there and doodle to my heart's content, usually drawings of tiny, well-dressed models in the margins of my notes. Halfway through the class, there was a sharp knock at the door. Most students looked up, but I continued drawing, not caring about what the day's lunch menu was or whatever the knocker was here for. Someone was being addressed, but it all sounded fuzzy to me. Listen? They were lucky I even showed up.

"Felicia!" a voice boomed sharply. I looked up into the eyes of my history teacher, pursing her pale, coral frosted lips at me. They completely clashed with her hot pink pantsuit, and I stifled a snicker as I responded innocently.

"Yes?"

"Here's a pass," she said, somewhat gruffly. "You're excused for the rest of class."

My first thought was one of joy, but then I remembered that there had to be some sort of reason behind the excuse, so I was instantly filled with suspicion. As I was ushered out of the room, the whispers began. I rolled my eyes at the immaturity, especially of an Honors class, but marched out with dignity. I don't know why I was acting like I was on trial or something, but I pretended like a camera crew was following me and taking note of my confident, indifferent expression.

"So, um, what's this for?" I asked the office aid, who clucked her tongue at me disapprovingly before answering.

In her turtleneck, big bouffant, and tweed slacks, she reminded me of a grandmother. "You're going to the counselor," she said, snapping her gum.

"But I don't want to go to the counselor," I said, hurrying to keep up with her quick strides.

"Too bad," she said, not seeming to care whether I kept up or not. We reached the counselor's office and she rapped on the door twice before opening it. Ugh. The last time I'd seen the counselor had been after Carrie's death, and all she'd done was offer me M&Ms and ask me to describe what I was feeling. She'd slip her glasses on, make careful notes in a little brown leather notebook and make the appropriate agreeable sound here and there. I hadn't gotten much out of the sessions and when I'd stopped coming, she hadn't contacted me so I figured everything was fine. So what was I doing here again?

"Felicia!" the counselor, Ms. Holmer, said, her voice oozing with sweetness. "It's so good to see you again!" She was young, fresh out of college, and had a short red pixie cut, which suited her small, heart-shaped face. She was short and covered in freckles, big-boned but so confident that she always looked great. She was somewhat hip, often wearing clothes that many of the girls in school would find themselves jealous of, but it seemed to me that she tried a little too hard. I was always suspicious of her.

"Why don't you close the door behind you?" she asked, flashing me a bright smile.

"So why am I here?" I asked bluntly, not bothering to sit down.

"Please, have a seat," she urged, unable to take the hint that my lingering by the door meant I didn't plan to stay.

I reluctantly sat on the edge of the chair, hoping she'd just explain it to me.

"Felicia," she began mysteriously, putting on her glasses (she always did this before she began to spout one of her speeches. Did they give her counselor super-powers or something?) "You've been referred to come here by some people who care about you dearly," she finished..

"Like who?" I asked. "For what?"

"Well, it seems as though they're a bit concerned about your eating habits," she said, looking my outfit up and down. "You do look much thinner than you did at our last meeting," she added, her eyes fixed on my body for an uncomfortably long period of time.

"Is that why I'm here?" I shouted, bolting up from my chair. "Why does everyone suddenly care about what I'm eating? Just because I'm not as skinny as my sister doesn't mean that I need help! I'm perfectly capable of losing weight on my own!"

"What?" Ms. Holmer asked, her voice shocked and somewhat scared. "Felicia, please calm down! You think someone recommended me to give you diet tips? Are you nuts?" she asked, losing formalities for a second.

"I'm tired of people talking to me about stuff that's none of their business!" I cried, pulling open the door and slamming it closed before stomping down the hallway.

"Hey!" the security guard shouted from the other end of the hall.

I ignored him and kept walking until I reached the main entrance, pushing the door and stepping out into daylight.

Chapter 43

The air was cold, but the sun felt like a blanket on my shivering shoulders, and I welcomed the brisk coolness, so different from the stuffy, warm, and suffocating atmosphere of the school. I hugged my arms to myself, somewhat comforted by the fact that I was wearing thick, heavy clothing that hid my body. The sky was grey and cloudy, projecting a thin mist that I couldn't really feel, but was visibly dampening my clothes. The weather reminded me of the day that Carrie and I really sort of split up.

It had been a day just like that. Cold, yet in a battle between sunny and cloudy. The sun would peek out for a moment, warming my skin, but would soon dart behind the clouds, making the sky dark and temperamental. School was over and Carrie was going to walk home, so I decided to accompany her rather than take the bus. As usual, she ignored me for most of the walk, instead talking on her cell phone to Jennifer, who was seriously standing like, twenty feet behind us. I rolled my eyes and started singing loudly and obnoxiously, hoping to annoy her enough that she would hang the phone up.

"Felicia!" she snapped, covering the mouthpiece of the phone. (Technically, it came out more like 'Ful-lee-see-yah'.) "Let me call you back, Jen," she said quickly, shoving the phone in her backpack and glaring at me.

"What?" I asked innocently. "I just felt like talking."

"About what?" she asked, sounding distracted and somewhat annoyed.

"Geez," I responded, hurt. "I didn't know it was a crime to want to talk to my sister."

"Well I have nothing to talk to you about," she quipped snidely, walking faster. She wore her cheerleader uniform with thick black tights, which sort of clashed with the whole outfit and did no job at hiding how painfully thin her legs were. The neck of the top sort of slid down to her collarbone, and she looked a little like a child playing grown-up in her mother's closet. I think of her now and can only think of how beautiful she looked.

"What is your problem?" I asked, nearly running now to keep up with her, huffing and puffing as though I were the third little pig. I wince now when I think about how out of shape I was. The new me could run the old me around the block.

"What's my problem?" she shrieked, stopping in place and turning to face me, her eyes wild and bloodshot and her hair tangled and thin, looking dry and not as glamorous as it usually did. She reminded me of some sort of villain from a movie, and I actually felt a little scared as she stood there, her fists clenched at her side.

"My problem," she retorted, "is that you won't ever leave me alone! Carrie, why didn't you eat your potatoes?" she mimicked in a whiny voice that apparently was supposed to be mine. "Carrie, I want to borrow your pants but they're too small on me. Carrie, why don't you talk to me in the lunchroom? Carrie, aren't you going to help me finish this ice cream? Carrie, what should I wear to school tomorrow?"

By this point, her breathing had become uneven and haggard, and her shoulders visibly moved up and down as she yelled, making it seem like she was about to explode.

"Don't you think," she finished, "that I have more important things in my life right now to worry about than you? Whatever you choose to wear to school is still probably going to look stupid, and the reason I don't want to help you finish the ice cream or eat my potatoes is because I don't want to look like you!"

The wind felt like it had been knocked out of me. I went cold all over, my clammy hands reaching up to grab my chest, sure that they would somehow stop my heart from spilling out. Did I truly look so disgusting to Carrie that she couldn't stand the thought of looking like me even though we were identical twins?

"I can't believe how mean you've become," I said quietly, quickly wiping the tears from my eyes before she could see that I was crying.

"Whatever," she said, turning her back on me to fish her phone out of her backpack so she could call her second-in-command back.

"I…I want a divorce from you!" I said angrily. "Or emancipation, whatever it is. From this moment on, you might be my twin, related to me by blood, but we are no longer sisters and we are no longer friends," I said dramatically, raising my chin in the air and stomping ahead of her.

I heard no reply, so I glanced back and saw that she had no expression on her face. She was looking in my direction, but she seemed to be looking through me. It was somewhat eerie, and I waved my hand in front of her face but she batted it away and kept walking.

"Um, are you going to answer me?" I asked, knowing that I'd already annoyed her beyond belief for the day.

"Oh, what? Are we friends again?" she snapped. "You may have forgotten the words you just spoke before, Fee, but we're not friends. I've grown up and you…well, I don't really know what it is that you've done, but as you oh so eloquently pointed out a minute ago, the only thing that keeps us together is that we were birthed from the same mother. So if you'd just shut up for one minute and go back to whining about how you don't have any friends and how I'm not a sister to you anymore, then maybe we can both be happy."

It was unbelievable how hurtful she could be in such a short time. I didn't know who this girl was, but it certainly wasn't Carrie. I remember crying, the cold air whipping my cheeks and making my skin feel raw. Ever since that day, things hadn't been the same between me and Carrie. Now that I think about it, things changed right around the time she started dieting and working out like a crazy person. I bet that sounds hypocritical, but I'm sure that she was one hundred times worse than me.

Chapter 44

By the time I got home, I felt restless but didn't want to work out my usual way. I decided to put my iPod on shuffle and dance around my room. It was relaxing for a while, almost somewhat fun. But at some point I shimmied myself past Carrie's dresser and picked up a picture of her that was taken about a month before she died. It was taken at one of the football games, and she looked beyond beautiful.

It was night, but a pale glow cast by moonlight shined on her face, making her skin look sparkly and fresh. Her eyes were tired, but the color was startlingly pretty, almost like a dark pool of rainwater. Her cheekbones were high and somewhat gaunt, but the carefully applied blush she wore made her look like someone who belonged in a magazine make-up ad. Her face was a lot thinner than it had been, but the sharp angles made her perfectly chiseled features look model-like. Her smile stretched across her face, and her lips curved into a perfect bow.

Suddenly, the Cure's "Why Can't I Be You" blared out of the speakers, and I almost dropped the frame. Great. Even my iPod was mocking me now. Feeling foolish, I glanced at the picture again, realizing that her smile looked somewhat forced, and her teeth had a weird tinge to them, almost the same the dentist noticed the other day. Her eyes were glowing, but there was something haunting about them, something that made her look slightly unnatural. A weird feeling took over my body. It's so difficult to describe, but it happened to me every once in a while, and I hated it.

It usually insinuated something odd going on with my friends, the day, or pretty much anything. This is probably about the fourth time I've had it since I began this diet and persisted in the name of Carrie, but as usual, I brushed it off and got back to my workout. I almost rejoiced in pride when I realized that I'd eaten nothing for the day. Those days were special, the best of days. There was no greater feeling than going to bed with an empty stomach and waking up with a stomach that was pancake-flat. Lately though, I noticed that my stomach was less concave and seemed to be pushing out a little even though the rest of me seemed to be pushing in. It was kind of annoying, but I just vowed to do more sit-ups.

The year anniversary of Carrie's death was coming up, and I wasn't prepared for it at all. The last few months had flown by, the focus on my diet and Carrie plan taking over all other thoughts. I hadn't even realized what the date was and literally felt blood drain from my face when I glanced over at the calendar. That means it had been almost a full eight months since I'd started my operation, and what did I have to show for it? Almost nothing.

Sure, a few people noticed I looked thinner but I know it wasn't the best I could look. I started feeling sorry for myself, and in a moment of panic and forgetfulness, I lunged for the phone and began dialing Julian's number, forgetting that I hadn't actually spoken to him in weeks and trying to ignore the painful reminder that he hadn't tried to speak to me.

I hung up after the phone rang once but then decided to call again for reasons I can't explain.

"Hello?" his deep voice came, almost too comforting. I remained silent, unable to speak. I had no idea what to say.

"Someone there?" he asked again, a slight twinge of irritation in his voice. Even though he had every right to be upset, the change of tone immediately made me wonder if I should hang up.

"Felicia, I have caller ID," he finally said, sounding slightly amused but more than a little annoyed.

"I'm sorry," I burst out.

"For what? I mean, there are a lot of things you could be sorry about, so which one is it?" he asked snippily, instantly pushing me away.

"Look, I know I haven't been the greatest friend to you," I began shakily, "but there are some things that I'm going through right now that I just can't get through alone."

The line was silent for a moment, and I winced, bracing myself for what was sure to come next.

"In case you forgot, I tried to be there for you since the very beginning, but all you've done is push me away and tell me that you can't be friends and hang out with the clones and that Josh loser."

"Josh is not a loser!" I objected.

"Yeah, sure, that's the part you pick out from that entire last statement. I'm pretty busy, Felicia, so what do you want?"

Suddenly I heard a soft giggle in the background. There was a rustling noise on the other end of the receiver, and Julian's muffled voice said, "Knock it off, will ya?" teasingly.

"Is Locker Girl with you?" I said boldly and with renewed anger.

"Who?" Julian asked, sounding genuinely confused.

"Oh, forget it!" I snapped, and hung up, fresh, hot tears sliding down my cheeks.

I stomped around my room for a minute before I realized that I'd done all of this myself. I suddenly felt angry at Carrie all over again.

"What have you done to me?" I bellowed, not caring if anyone heard me. "I'm covered in hair and bruises, I have no friends, and I'm still fat!" I crowed, laughing hysterically now.

I hadn't gotten my period in three months now. My nails were brittle and yellow, and they reminded me of the nails of an old lady who didn't choose to groom herself. My hair had become thin and my eyes looked sunken in. Never mind the fact that I didn't believe the scale, which earlier read 88. That number was way too low, and from the mirror's version of these thunder thighs which probably weighed about 40 pounds each, there was no way it was real.

"I hate this life!" I shrieked, my dramatic side allowing the tantrum to take over me. I started kicking my bed and suddenly got the inspiration to break my mirror. It'd be like a scene out of a movie. But I didn't want to have to clean that up. After ranting and raving with no one to stop me for a few more minutes, I sat at the foot of the bed, feeling more exhausted than I had in days. Suddenly, something hit me in the head, hard.

"Ouch!" I yelled aloud, again not caring that no one heard me since nobody cared anyway. I reached to the side of me and picked up the object, realizing that it was a diamond encrusted miniature rabbit's foot. Of course the diamonds were fake, but it was beautiful to look at. A very eerie sensation came over me and my eyes flew to the picture of Carrie on the desk, which seemed to be gazing back at me. I clutched at my heart and tried to stand up, but that paralyzing feeling I'd experienced on the couch had come back. I couldn't move no matter how hard I tried.

The rabbit's foot had last been seen inside of Carrie's jewelry box. It was the lucky charm she used to soothe herself when she was feeling bad. I'd wanted to put it inside her casket, but a selfish part of me thought maybe the luck would work for me too. I felt terrified at that moment, wondering how the rabbit's foot had gotten out of the box. Maybe when I was kicking things around, the box fell on its side and the foot fell out. My eyes rolled heavenward to glance at the box's position, which was still upright. I started breathing hard and wanted to get out of that room. It's not that I was afraid of ghosts or my sister, but whatever had just happened, it wasn't settling right with me. I knew that I was just unnecessarily scaring myself, so I raced out of the room and fell asleep downstairs.

Chapter 45

Time went by but I wasn't counting days anymore. I felt sick all the time. It seemed like I had a cold I could never get rid of, and I'd started layering my clothes at school even though it had gotten a bit warmer out. Forget fashion. I suddenly looked like a crazy bag lady. My warmest pair of sweatpants was bright purple and very baggy on me, so they hid my thighs. I'd nicknamed myself "Large and in Charge" in my head, and liked to repeat the mantra to myself as I marched down the hallways. I never really ran into Julian at school, which was somewhat comforting, but part of me still had hope that he'd try to find me.

I couldn't concentrate in school at all anymore. I'd filled almost an entire notebook with recordings of what I'd eaten in the last six months. In the beginning, the lists were fairly long, filled with lots of fruits and vegetables. Now, they tended to include only water and sometimes nothing. I'd gotten to the same point Carrie had. Even if I wanted to eat, I didn't feel like it anymore. I was somewhat concerned about not getting my period, but I was more concerned about my stomach.

I'd finally noticed some changes in my arms and legs, but my stomach always appeared to be bloated and stuck out a little, no matter how many sit-ups and crunches I did. That was just weird. I stopped bothering to wear makeup to school anymore. My face had grown pale and my eyes were constantly rimmed with deep blue and purple. Surprisingly, my tormenters stopped paying me much attention. The other day, I accidentally bumped into Allison, and rather than push me or yell at me, she opened her mouth to say something but quickly stopped, shaking her head at me. The strange thing was, I saw pity in her eyes, and I didn't like that. Who was she to pity me?

Things were terrible at school, and they were just as bad at home. I don't think I'd seen my mother in weeks. No one was there to sign forms from my teachers that explained that I was on the verge of failing. No one was there to monitor my eating or pay attention to whether I was doing alright. No one was there to stop me from looking in the mirror and telling myself it just wasn't enough. I wasn't blind. Of course I noticed that I had lost weight, but it still wasn't enough. I was never thin enough, and I'd gone so long without eating that I don't think it was even working anymore. I'd never be like Carrie. She was graceful in her thinness; I just looked gawky and odd.

"Felicia!" my dad's voice shouted one night, rousing me from my "thinspiration" searches. As silly as it sounded, I often searched the Internet for pictures of thin women so that I could feel inspired and work even harder towards my goal. There were lots of supportive groups, and it had become a nightly thing for me.

"What?" I yelled back, too tired to get up and actually go to him.

"Come here," he called back, forcing me to get up anyway. I groaned and stood up, and when I did, my pants slipped down around my waist, angering me. I didn't have any pants smaller than this, and I couldn't have lost that much weight. They were just stretched out, I decided. I felt dizzy walking down the stairs, and when I put my hand to my forehead, it was cold as ice. I ignored my tiredness as usual and padded into the living room.

"Yes?" I asked my father, who sat in front of the television watching a basketball game, his papers gathered in a stack on the coffee table in front of him. His opened briefcase was at his feet, revealing another stack of papers. He looked thoroughly absorbed in the game and barely glanced up as I came into the room.

"Can you run into my office and grab me a folder marked Case 138, please?" he asked, his eyes never straying from the television. I was about to complain until I noticed that he was handing me his key ring.

"Sure!" I said excitedly, practically snatching it from his hand. My tiredness suddenly faded, and I raced upstairs with a new lightness. I got into the office and shut the door, and the first thing I did was try each of the keys on the file cabinet. When I found the right one, I casually took it off the key ring and slipped it into my sweatpants pocket. After grabbing the folder he'd requested, I bounded down the stairs and handed it to him.

"Thanks, hon," he said, putting the key ring back onto his belt loop without examining it. *Tonight*, I thought.

Chapter 46

It seemed like I waited forever for him to finally go to bed, especially since he works so late on cases. I drifted in and out of sleep a few times, but each time I felt the smooth, cold metal of the key in my hand, I was jerked awake. When the house was silent and dark, I crept from my bedroom into the hallway, careful to make it to the office without making too much noise. When I finally got there, my stomach twisted in half, and my head was filled with fear.

I prayed that my father wasn't having an affair, that he wouldn't leave me alone with my mother, which really would simply be leaving me alone. I pushed myself forward. My hand was trembling, so it took a couple tries before I inserted the key correctly. The click should have been satisfying, but instead it just terrified me even more. I'd waited so long for this moment, so long to catch my father in the act that I now wished I could almost put the key back and go back to my blissful ignorance. Well, I couldn't quite call it blissful since I'd always suspected something, but I was still scared.

With shaking hands, I leafed through the folders, desperate to find something that would prove my efforts hadn't been wasted. I stopped when I came across a folder marked Casablancas, Carrie. I knew that my dad had folders for each of us, but this one was oddly thick in comparison to mine and Andrew's. Curiously, I opened it, wondering what he had on her that he didn't have on us. I browsed through the papers, passing over school files and old doctor files until I came to one that almost made my heart stop.

It was marked with a date of death, and there were records from the hospital along with audits from the police and physicians. This was odd, I thought to myself. The last paper in the stack was her death certificate, and even though I already knew what it said, something drew me to it. I glanced at it briefly, but something caught my eye. The certificate read: "Cause of Death: Car Accident/Heart Attack," but there was a special note next to it that indicated that the majority death cause was from an eating disorder but death certificates didn't cite eating disorders as causes.

"What?" I said out loud, smacking my hand over my mouth. "Heart attack?" I started furiously paging through the documents, each one worse than the last.

One of them was an audited conversation from the doctor, who said that Carrie was alive when she arrived at the hospital and would have lived if not for complications due to her eating disorder. Another document described the accident, explaining that Carrie suffered from low potassium and endured a minor heart attack that forced her to lose control of the wheel and hit another driver. She'd blacked out at the wheel.

How could this be? How could her eating disorder be that bad? How could it even be classified as an eating disorder? We all knew that she had issues with eating and was having weight problems, but this couldn't have caused death, could it? If these documents are real, that means my sister could have lived if she hadn't stopped eating. That means that my parents lied to my brother and me.

"No!" I howled furiously, sinking to my knees on the plush carpet.

"No," I whimpered, my head leaning back against the cold metal of the file cabinet I wished I'd never gone through. I started sobbing, promising that I'd give or do anything if I could just go back in time to one year ago. Had I known that Carrie would have died because she had stopped eating, I'd have never left her side. I'd have forced food down her throat and made her see that it was all a mistake.

A light bulb went off—her friends! Jennifer and Allison and all of their ridiculous minions are the ones that made Carrie this way! I had to enact revenge. I had to do something. A guttural roar came out of me, and I found myself clawing at the file cabinets in anger. Something was coming over me and there was no way to control it.

I began gasping for air, punching things and knocking the papers out of my way, in disbelief that this had been kept from us for so long. As far as Andrew and I knew, she had died because of the car accident. No one ever told us it was from an eating disorder. I think back and I knew that things weren't right with her. I knew that she had some problems, but I guess I never went so far to think that she actually had a disorder. And to think she had a heart attack at the age of 17!

My vision became blurry with tears when I realized how little I really knew my sister. How could I have missed all the signs? Shouldn't it have been part of my responsibility to watch her and make sure she was okay? How could my parents feel fine with telling us and everyone else that it was from the car accident? Unable to do anything else, I let out a bloodcurdling scream and pulled my knees up to my chest, wrapping my arms around my legs and rocking back and forth in pain, knowing that there was nothing I could do to make it go away.

Chapter 47

A light turned on in the hallway and for some reason I felt scared, knowing that whoever was out there was someone I couldn't trust. I whimpered and burrowed further into my little cocoon, squeezing my eyes shut and praying that whoever it was would go away and leave me to lie like this forever. Footsteps scurried across the hallway and the door banged open with a thud.

"Felicia!" my dad yelled. "What's wrong? What happened?"

He saw me lying on the floor with the folder in my hand and a look of pain washed across his face. He knelt down next to me and took the papers out of my hand, tossing them in the corner of the room before folding my body into his arms. We both shook with sobs, and he brushed the hair off my forehead and began humming a song that he had always sung to Carrie and me when we were children.

Off-key but meaning well, he started singing:

My two little girls mean the world to me.

My two little girls so different but free.

Alone and separate until we meet

Together at last under God's tree.

It was a silly little rhyme that he'd made up that never really meant too much to either my sister or me in terms of lyrics, but it hit me so hard now that I was almost unable to contain myself. Even though it seemed obvious now, the words had never connoted death for me. They simply reminded me of going our separate ways in school and meeting up underneath the large tree in our backyard, a tree which we endearingly referred to as God's tree since the top of it was rounded like a halo and allowed light from the heavens to shine through on a sunny day.

The words seemed harsh but were more comforting than my father probably knew. I hated him and needed him at the same time. Still, I could not stop crying. I cried so hard that I couldn't breathe, and my chest heaved with the effort to stop wheezing. At one point, I thought I had to vomit, but there was no food inside of me and I could only dry-heave, which was extremely painful, causing heartburn and discomfort.

My dad stared at me, his eyes glistening with tears. He seemed lost at that moment, and even though I was beyond mad at him, part of me wanted to comfort him too. Grizzly poked his head in the door, mistaking us actually being together for family time, bounding over to us and staring expectantly, but settling at our feet when he realized things were tense.

We sat in silence for a few more minutes, and just as he was opening his mouth to speak, the door creaked open and my mother peered in, her face tight and tired but also worried. She was so small and so quiet that we hadn't even heard her pad across the hallway. She took one look at me curled up in my father's arms like a baby and the tears started spilling out of her eyes too.

I expected her to rush out of the room and retreat to her safe place, but she surprised us both by hesitantly kneeling down next to us. Her lips were shaking with the effort to not double over in sobs, and in that moment, I saw one of the most beautiful sights imaginable. My dad reached out his large bear paw of a hand, his wedding ring gleaming under the hint of moonlight streaming through the window. Slowly, my mom extracted her small, fragile hand from the folds of her nightgown and reached out too, her matching gold band glittering with his simultaneously. When their hands connected, he pulled her into our circle and fiercely wrapped his arms around her, kissing the top of her head and pulling me closer into his chest. We sat in unity for a moment, our arms gripping each other tight, almost as though we were only now registering how long we'd been away from each other and were afraid that if we let go, we'd get lost all over again.

I wasn't happy with my parents, and I certainly wasn't going to forgive them for lying to me, but I'd been waiting for a hug, to be yelled at, anything that would make them reach out, and this was the first time I'd gotten it in months. Finally, my father shifted gears, and for a second, I thought I was face-to-face with my sister.

I stared in horror at the girl that looked back at me through my father's glassy TV. She was gaunt and tired-looking, almost ghoul-like. The bags under her eyes seemed to stretch down for miles, and her cheekbones were so hollow that they could probably catch something in them. The eyes were distant and sad, devoid of light and warmth, and the hair was stringy, unhealthy, and thin. This is how my sister had looked in her last few days of living. This is how I looked now.

Chapter 48

I don't know what was more shocking to me. My parents were both with me at the same time, and we were all holding one another. I'd also just looked at myself in the mirror and saw a girl who was completely different from the one I'd seen in the mirror earlier. I was puzzled at how quickly things had changed, but I was even more horrified at what I saw. Was that really how I looked? As if reading my thoughts, my mother started to clutch at the bones in my back, gripping the sharp edges and raking her hands down my ribcage as if she were playing the piano. Fresh tears started to brew in her eyes and all at once I both hated myself for making her go through this all over again and hated her for abandoning me when I needed her the most.

My dad was the first one to speak up. "We all need to talk," he said slowly, his voice tired and gravelly.

We retreated to the kitchen, where my dad halfheartedly whipped up a batch of his hot chocolate. He always put in real dark chocolate and even sometimes whipped the cream himself. Tonight though, it was made quickly. After he set three steaming mugs on the table, we all put our hands over the tops of the cups, warming them and unsure of what to say.

"Felicia," my dad finally said, "We owe you an apology. We should have told you everything about your sister's death. You have to understand how shocked we were at the time, though."

"Yes," my mother echoed, her voice quiet and distant, her eyes unable to meet anything but the inside of her mug. "I couldn't believe that I had managed to miss the fact that my daughter had anorexia. She was so thin -- too, too thin, but she was always hiding in those baggy clothes. I honestly thought she'd gone on a silly health kick. I did something similar in high school. Just a little diet to look good in uniform. But it wasn't just a little diet. And I, as a mother, failed to see it. I couldn't admit that I'd done that. And I couldn't lose you and Andrew in the same way. I was trying to protect you."

It was the most I think I'd heard my mother say at one time in months. It was a lot to take in, and even though it sounded selfish, for some strange reason, a part of me understood. Yet I failed to see how protecting us meant ignoring Andrew while he was away at school and leaving me to fend for myself during some of the most important times in my life.

Slowly, it began to sink in that I was no longer an A student. I didn't have the same grades I used to, I wasn't involved in the same activities, and I barely had friends. I don't know what I'd let happen to me, but part of me resented my parents for letting it happen too.

"What about those secret phone calls?" I blurted out, desperate to stop myself from thinking about all the ways I'd managed to screw up my life in the past few months. My dad raised an eyebrow, a genuinely confused look on his face.

"You know, those calls in your office late at night and the letter and stuff," I said quickly, becoming louder as I spoke. "That's what I went into your office for in the first place! I want to know why you're telling people not to call here and getting perfumed letters in the mail!"

I slammed down my mug as I finished the statement, and cocoa sloshed onto the table. My mother shot me a disapproving look, which normally would be considered a bad thing, but to me, it was an incredibly positive sign. She had noticed something I'd done and it bothered her!

"I noticed you two fighting," I continued. "Dad, you were always hiding what you were doing. And Mom, you were yelling at Dad for leaving the house in the middle of the night!"

My mom and dad met each other's eyes across the table, and my dad let out a heavy sigh before holding his hands up in surrender.

"Look, Felicia, there isn't any doubt that the death of a child obviously creates a struggle in relationships. Yes, your mother and I have had some pretty grave problems over the last few months.

However, I wasn't doing anything that would constitute our marriage," my dad said.

"You weren't having an affair?" I croaked, feeling the wind knock out of me, except I felt relief instead of pain. All that time I'd spent worrying and determined to be a detective was silly, but I am slightly glad I pursued it, although it lead me to something that I wish I could have continued not knowing about.

"No!" my father exclaimed. "You think I would do that?" he almost spat, fury and disbelief in his voice.

"Adrian," my mother chided softly. My father, the big strong man, had a tendency to act very childish when he was accused of something he didn't do. The lawyer in him would disappear and he'd suddenly be a 5-year-old again, stamping around the house screaming, "I didn't do it!" My mother had always been able to calm him down, and I was glad she still could.

"This is tough for me to admit, but I've been seeing a therapist for quite some time after Carrie...passed away," my dad said, burying his face in his hands for a moment. "I know you guys have constantly thought of me as the reliable one who could take care of things for the family, and I felt sick that I couldn't do that anymore. I'd suddenly lost my position. I wasn't sleeping or eating. I even stopped going to work for a while, all of which I know you're unaware of. I finally decided that I needed some help. But I didn't want you and Andrew to lose sight of who I was to you."

He looked out the window for a minute, his eyes growing cloudy.

"I started to go to a therapist about five months ago. The therapist has also directed me to a support group for parents whose children have died of eating disorders. Everything was kept so secret because I didn't want you or Andrew to know. I know we were wrong to lie to you. I know that. But like your mother said, all we wanted to do was protect you."

My eyes were fixated on the wall behind his head, and I was almost unable to comprehend anything he said.

"How do you explain the tan?" I asked lamely, unable to think of anything else to say.

"The uh, therapy includes, um, spa sessions," he coughed, his eyes

167

roaming around the room.

At this, my mother smirked and let out a tiny chuckle. This was the first spark of life I'd seen in my mother in as long as I could remember. My lips curled up a little and a tiny laugh came out. Then my father laughed a giant guffaw. Soon we were all laughing hysterically, these loud, unusual sounds bellowing from deep within our stomachs, and had tears streaming down our faces. It was the first happy moment we'd shared together in months, and just for a second, I believed that everything was going to be okay. Then I caught a flash of my reflection in the chrome toaster and realized that it wasn't.

"Maybe I needed one of you to take me aside and yell at me every once in a while. Tell me that I wasn't looking too great lately and you weren't going to stand for it. Maybe Carrie needed that too," I said softly.

I was afraid that my mother was going to start weeping again, so I put my hand tentatively over hers to show her that I wasn't being accusatory.

"I know," she said, releasing a heavy sigh and bowing her head to rub her eyes. "I don't even know who I am anymore," she said quietly, pushing her chair back and getting up to leave.

"No!" I admonished firmly, standing up and forcefully bringing her arm back down. "All you've been doing these last few months is running away!" I cried, my voice beginning to sound hoarse. "Do you realize this last hour is probably the most I've seen you in combined time since Carrie died? You might not know who you are, but these are the first signs of you showing that you're still an actual person!" I yelled bluntly, somewhat breathless.

My dad sat silently observing in the background, his hands placed beneath his chin with a perplexed look on his face.

"You don't know what it is like," my mother said finally.

"I know that I don't know what it's like to lose a child, but you have to remember that I know what it's like to lose a sister," I responded. "So if I don't know what it's like, then help me see, and let me help you," I urged, the words coming out of my mouth so fast I wasn't even sure what I was saying.

"If that's the way you feel, then you also have to let us help you," my dad interjected, a pleading look on his face.

"There's nothing wrong with me," I scoffed, but the words were unbelievable even to me. The face in the mirror of the toaster seemed to taunt me, smirking at my denial. But I couldn't lie to myself.

Something had sparked within me when I had seen the words on that paper. At one point, they'd all blurred together: death, eating disorder, heart attack. I admitted that they had a grave impact on me. Suddenly, becoming skinnier seemed scarier. My head had snapped up after reading the words, and my mind swam through everything I'd experienced in the last few months. The body hair, bruises, paralysis, tooth decay, and fainting spells all seemed so insignificant when paired next to death. At the same time, they seemed realer than ever. I knew I could no longer go about living like that when I knew now that it was a matter of life and death.

Chapter 49

Still, it wasn't as easy to change as I assumed it would be. My hot chocolate sat in front of me untouched, and even though it smelled sweet and inviting, my head automatically added up to the calories and my brain told me to push it away. Although I hadn't been operating with too much logic lately, I did realize that it was a little unfair to try to convince my parents to take my help when I was pushing theirs away.

I was thinking of a way to politely tell them to back off when my dad came next to me and lightly caught my wrist. He pushed the sleeve of my oversized sweatshirt up and held my arm out to my mother, who gasped.

"What?" I asked, somewhat annoyed, trying to yank my hand out of his grasp. But before I could, he held my arm up to the light and I thought I was possibly seeing what my parents saw. The arm was small, almost too small to call delicate. The bones stuck out at odd angles, the elbow sharply protruding. The arm was dotted with small bruises, marching up my arm like a cobalt and wine constellation. It was not very attractive, and it closely mirrored the condition of Carrie's arm in her last few days. I don't know how I was able to see it now and hadn't been able to see it before. It was almost as though not eating had become a drug for me, one that distorted everything I was able to see. Or maybe I just chose not to see it.

"My baby!" my mom cried, grabbing my arm and awkwardly patting it. Then she started grabbing my shoulders, back, and legs, pinching at the bones and making noises of disapproval. I'm surprised she didn't whip out a tape measure and start wrapping it around my waist. I wanted to shrug her off of me, but as pathetic as it sounds, the fact that she'd called me her "baby," something I hadn't heard in months, forced me to allow her to do whatever she wanted.

Suddenly, her eyes became wild, and she stood up and started pacing back and forth. My dad and I stared at her for a moment. We seemed almost fascinated, as though we were visiting a zoo and watching a tiger pad back and forth in its secluded mini-jungle. She made a beeline for the sink and reached beneath it, removing a small spray bottle of bleach and a red rag, which was really just an old tee-shirt of my dad's cut in half. She began spraying the counter and scrubbing with all the vigor of a marathon runner, muttering to herself.

"What are you doing?" my dad asked, traces of amusement and worry in his voice. She stopped scrubbing for a moment and looked up, almost as though she'd forgotten we were in the room. Her eyes narrowed a bit, but it wasn't an angry look, just one that was deep in thought.

When she finally answered, her voice was calm but determined. "I already lost one daughter. I'm not going to lose another one."

Her tone lacked the distance that she'd carried with her the last few months. Part of me wanted to jump up and dance and scream, "She's back!" However, I knew it was not that easy. My mother may have been livelier than she'd been in months, but there was still a lot of healing that each of us needed to do, both together and alone. The woman had left me to get through life alone after my twin had died. She hadn't cared about my schoolwork, the issues I was going through, or noticed that my body was conforming to my sister's, and there was a lot of intense hurt that came along with that.

My excitement at my mother's claim on me was short-lived, though. I was still scared to let my Carrie transformation go, even though I now knew the consequences. I had worked so hard on it for so long. It had been all that mattered to me, and I wasn't sure if I could let it go just like that. The documents in Carrie's file had been strong, strong enough to force me to wake up, and the glimpse of myself in the mirror had almost been stronger, but there was still something inside me that was terrified to let go of what had become my life.

171

Let it go. I jumped, looking around the room wildly. A voice had interrupted my internal debate, and if I was not mistaken, it had said, "Let it go." I wondered for a minute if it had been me or Carrie. Our voices sounded surprisingly similar, although hers usually had a snappier tone and weird inflection that she'd started using ever since she'd become friends with the "nimrods," as I liked to call them.

I was spooked, almost as scared as I was when the rabbit foot had fallen on me, but there was also a sense of calm that washed over me. For once, my limbs didn't feel like they were vibrating with anxiety. At that moment, my stomach let out a loud gurgle that sounded almost like a howl.

My parents looked at each other and smiled slightly. The next thing I knew, they were next to each other and reaching up into the cabinets and pulling down mixing bowls and measuring cups. My mother, who was a lot shorter than my father, put her hands on her hips and pointed at things she needed, and he gladly obliged her. Soon, the room was filled with the sounds of clanking metal, the sizzle of a frying pan, and the cracking of eggs.

The aroma of bacon, sweet scent of pancakes, and fresh potatoes wafted through the air, causing my stomach to groan even more angrily than it had before. I was shocked. My parents were making breakfast for dinner, something we hadn't done in months. Technically, it was close to morning, but it was still surprising to see the old tradition.

They worked together fluidly, going through the motions as though they did it every day. Even though the kitchen was devoid of conversation, I did see the glances they shot each other, and it wasn't hard to see the love that was still there. I was somewhat ashamed that I'd been so convinced my father was having an affair, but the signs were there. I guess I could understand how a marriage might be strained after a child dies, but the whole thing was still a little confusing to me.

The sight of my parents together and the familiar scents of a loving kitchen were all so comforting me that my eyes began to feel heavy. I tilted my head to the side and let my eyes close, but before I could drift off, I heard the beginning of an upbeat song and felt a grin curl over my lips. "A Little Respect" by Erasure filled the kitchen, and I looked up and saw both of my parents smiling at me, their eyebrows raised in invitation.

My parents had both been very into 80s music, one of the reasons that I loved older obscure artists so much. This song happened to be their wedding song, and as silly as it was, I could instantly picture the video we'd watched at least a thousand times—my father twirling my mother around and around and their faces lit brighter than Christmas trees—and the sound was something that resonated within all of us and always would. I shook my shoulders to the side a little, mimicking the awkward dancing that my dad had done in the video, and he whipped a dishtowel at me in mock fury.

As fun as this all was, it was also a bit surreal. Who knew that I'd be rewarded for going into my father's office and looking through his private files without permission? And why had it taken me acting inappropriately for them to change? Why couldn't they have just looked at me? I was so confused by all of it, but I was also terrified of losing my parents again. Still, the question needed to be asked.

"I want to know...what she said before she died," I said carefully, willing my parents to keep their lighthearted behavior but be honest with me. I needed to know.

Chapter 50

The smiles vanished from their faces. My dad set down his spatula and wiped his hands, abandoning his frying pan. My mother's face grew slightly pale and she started biting her nails, which was very unusual for her to do. She set the oven heat to low and glided gracefully to the table, a far cry from the way she'd been walking for the past few months. Sometimes she'd remind me of a grandmother the way she'd hobble.

"I know this is going to be hard for your mother to handle, so I guess I'll do some of the talking," my father said. My mother reached over and squeezed his hand gratefully, her ashen face slowly regaining some color.

"Carrie died very soon after we got to the hospital. When we got the call, all we'd been told was that she was in an accident. It wasn't until we got there that we'd learned she'd suffered a heart attack from having an eating disorder. We were both in denial. It wasn't easy to believe that a seventeen-year-old girl had experienced a heart attack. We both wanted to see her."

His voice was starting to shake, and he gripped the edge of the table so hard that his hands turned white. My mother continued to bite her nails, her eyes far from the room.

"When we got in there, neither of us knew who the girl in the bed was. She was so small, she looked as though she were an adolescent, malnourished boy. She was so pale that her skin was almost blue, and her face was heavily bruised. She had to summon all of her strength just to say a few words."

For once, my complete attention was on him. There were absolutely no distractions. It wasn't just something I wanted to hear—I *needed* to hear what he was going to say next.

"Her eyes lit up when we walked into the room. She didn't move any body parts, just stared at us. It was somewhat eerie, and your mother rushed over to her and started hugging her. We asked her to tell us what happened, but she didn't speak. Finally, she moved her lips, which were so dry and cracked that it was almost difficult to understand her. She said, 'I love you. I never meant for it to get this far.' Then she closed her eyes."

At the point, my mother started crying silently, her lips trembling and hands shaking as she reached for my father's hand again.

"It took a few minutes, but she opened her eyes again. She said, 'Tell Felicia I love her. Tell her that this isn't worth it. Tell her that in my book, she's the coolest girl.' She then closed her eyes again. We reached for her, shook her a little, but there was no more. She was gone."

I was stunned. It was hard for me to move, let alone speak. So I decided not to, incredulously wondering why they didn't think it was important to tell me this. I wanted more than anything to slam my hand down on the counter and make a dramatic exit, but the entire evening had simply drained all of my energy. Maybe it was time to turn the tables on them.

I calmly pushed my chair out, got up, pushed it back in, and started up the stairs without looking back. I could hear worried murmurs in the kitchen, but after I'd gone into my room and locked the door, there was silence. Within the next few hours, I drifted off to sleep once or twice only to be awakened by some timid knocks. At first, I'd start to get up, but then all of the events came rushing back and all I could do was curl my knees up to my stomach and beg to fall asleep again.

At one point, I really needed some water, so I opened the door and was met with a tray holding dishes that were part of the special blue china dining set. The plate was laden with fluffy French toast, cut into sticks like when I was a child. Next to the toast was a pile of golden scrambled eggs, which now looked dry and almost made me dry-heave at the sight. They were covered with crispy bacon. A tall glass of orange juice stood next to the plate, accompanied by a thin vase holding a wilted flower. It was a nice touch, but it certainly wasn't going to make me crawl downstairs for apologies. I simply pushed the tray aside untouched, filled my cup with water from the bathroom and retreated back to my bedroom, where I fell into a dreamless sleep.

Chapter 51

There was no way I was going to school the next morning. I opened my eyes before my preset alarm clock went off and pulled the plug out. It pained me to get out of my fuzzy cocoon, but I pulled the drapes shut and stacked some boxes against my door to make sure my parents wouldn't try to come in. Pulling a downy pillow over my head, I snuggled further into the little burrow I'd set up and fell back to sleep, not waking up again until the late afternoon.

I really didn't want to get out of bed. Whenever I'd woken up, I'd wrapped my arms around my stomach and prayed to God to take me away too. I wasn't suicidal; it was just hard to live with the fact that my parents had been lying to me, my sister may not have been as distant from me as I'd thought, and I'd somehow set my body into self-destruct mode. There was only one person who could help me right now, and that was Carrie.

There were so many questions left unanswered, so many things that I was desperate to understand. It wasn't the best source of comfort, but it'd have to do. I found myself digging out her diary, surprised that it had been a while since I looked at it. I'd always been scared of reading the last page, terrified that I would lose her after I'd finished the journal, but there was a part of me that felt that was the most important page for me to look at right now.

Every day I see darkness. Things have changed so drastically for me that it's difficult to even gather enough strength to write this. When I walk, things are hazy in my vision, and I can't explain it. My hands are constantly shaking, as though I've just drunk 5 cups of coffee. I'm always cold, no matter how many layers I put on, and it honestly hurts when anyone touches me. I feel like a fragile old lady. I look in the mirror and see weird patchy spots of fuzz on my face, almost like I'm morphing into some kind of animal. It's so hard to hide now. My friends are beginning to get suspicious at my refusal to eat during lunch or when we go out. My parents are becoming more accusatory, and my sister has even begun following me around. I really never, ever wanted it to be like this. I'm not happy with who I've become. I can visibly SEE that I'm way too thin, but my body has changed to the body I WANTED to have. It rejects food. I can't eat anything without throwing it up. I'm repulsed by the sight of food, and I've constantly got the chills and shakes. It seems like there isn't even a point in going on. I've become trapped in my body, which doesn't even allow me to do anything anymore. I couldn't escape it if I tried. I might look pretty, or sickly, as Allison once put it, but if I could go back in time, I'd definitely change this. Tonight, I'm going to break up with Peter. He's been so unsupportive through the entire thing, urging me to lose weight and caring more about my looks than anything else. He's also dull and really not funny at all. Josh, on the other hand, has been calling me lately. I'm not exactly cheating on Peter, but Josh has been so comforting and knows just the rights things to say. He even told me that he thought I could use a good hamburger, so I'm going to meet him there tonight. So glad I can drive now. I really wouldn't want my mother to drop me off and come inside and start asking questions. Maybe, just maybe my body will allow me to eat and behave like a normal girl.

I hadn't even realized that tears had been building in my eyes during reading. Even though this didn't answer my specific questions, there were some indirect answers in there. I almost felt a little bad for Josh, and reminded myself to thank him for being such a good friend. I'd never really liked Peter; he'd always reminded me of a rat with his squinty eyes and odd, upper lip hair that he'd insisted was a mustache.

The most important parts of the journal were the ones that I could relate to. I couldn't believe the same things had been happening to her and none of us had noticed. I guess it goes to show how easy it is to get caught up in a busy life. Around this time, Dad had just made partner and Mom was spending a lot of time freelancing for garden blogs and magazines. She'd studied journalism in college, and though she had steady work at a close public relations firm for the community newspapers, when she did freelance, she never really paid attention to anything but her old horticulture textbooks and garden. Andrew had been starting his first year at university, and...I don't really know what I was doing. I was always lost in my own world, I guess. My dad sometimes called me Alice, as in Alice in Wonderland, because I was always so curious. Yet this was an area that my inability to see what was going on around me clearly hadn't helped.

It was amazing to me that we'd all missed such a significant portion of Carrie's life. How had she walked past us every day, just skin and bones without us realizing it? I could understand, in a sense, how my mother felt like a failure. I felt the same. It seemed almost irrational that I could get so angry at them for failing to notice me when I hadn't even noticed this disease taking over my own sister. I was reluctant to call whatever was affecting me a disease, but after reading this last journal entry, taking another look in the mirror, and seeing the devastation of my parents, I realized there was something about me that needed to change. I wasn't about to open the door and scarf down the French toast, but I was somewhat prepared to forgive my parents and save myself before it was too late.

Chapter 52

I fell asleep clutching Carrie's journal in my arms. I heard soft knocks on my door throughout the day, but I chose to ignore them. Since my parents had shut me out for so long, it didn't bother me too much to do the same to them. I felt disgusting. I hadn't showered in a couple days, there was no food in me whatsoever, and my hair hung in greasy clumps, the strands stringy and thin. My hair used to be one of my best features. It was always thick, shiny, and soft.

As I lay in my own filth, I wonder how I'd let this happen to me. Then I wondered how Carrie had done the same. I realized that it wasn't exactly something I could control. While it first had been entirely about being in control, my power later slipped away from me. In the beginning, I enjoyed nothing more than being able to eat whatever I wanted and then rid myself of it. Nothing felt better than crawling into bed having ingested nothing but water for the entire day.

As odd as it sounds, the growl of my stomach was such a welcoming sound and sensation that I began to crave it. It was the only way I could feel good. Soon though, I couldn't control anything anymore. After a while, whenever I ate large quantities of food, my body reacted negatively. Since it was so used to losing the food, it was almost as though it had become self-programmed to reject whatever I'd put into it. Later, I'd begin to hate the smell and even sight of food.

I had gotten so much sleep in the past few days that when I shut my eyes, I couldn't drift away again. However, my body felt so weak and fragile that when I even attempted a sit-up, it almost collapsed involuntarily. Unable to do anything, I sat on the edge of my head, my head feeling dizzy and my vision fuzzy. Nothing was important to me anymore.

As I contemplated whether or not I should continue to take my diet pills (I'd started taking four per day, even though the label said not to exceed two, figuring it might help me lose twice as much weight), I heard a sharp rap on the door followed by a more timid knock. I ignored it, still reluctant to answer my parents after I'd felt betrayed for so long. I rubbed my eyes and yawned, certain that they'd give up and go back downstairs. This time was different. I heard the scratching of a key being inserted into my lock and the click of it opening.

"Hey!" I protested angrily. "Haven't you heard of knocking? How do you know I was decent?"

"We did knock," my mother said, breezing into the room with my father on her tail. "And I'm your mother; it's not like I haven't seen it all before."

My parents stormed to my bed and bombarded me. I made a move to get up, but my mom grabbed my arms and my dad grabbed my legs.

"What are you doing?" I yelled. "I'm going to report you for child abuse!"

"Nice try, kiddo," my dad said, sitting on my ankles.

"Ouch!" I whined, annoyed. "Can you guys just get out of here, please?" I guess I had forgotten that I wasn't supposed to be talking to them.

"We see what you're doing, Felicia," my mom said softly, getting serious. She reached forward and carefully brushed a strand of hair out of my eyes. I felt bad for her, as it probably left a streak of grease on her finger.

"We're not going to stand for it," my dad continued, releasing my ankles and resting a hand on my leg. He winced as he felt the bone, and I could see his determination shrink just a little in his face. He refused to give up, though, as he maintained what he'd been saying.

"I know that we've been unfair to you in the past few months. Your mother and I have been having a lot of difficulty just being ourselves, let alone being parents. But we've realized that we've been going about this the entirely wrong way."

"He's right," my mother chimed in, resting her chin in her hand.

She gazed at me in adoration, despite my weak and gross condition, and there was a light in her eyes that had been gone for so long that I wanted to catch it inside of a bottle and keep it there forever in case it ever went missing again.

"We've had a lot of time to talk in the last couple days. I see how out of it I was. Unpaid bills were stacked up on the table. The house was so dirty that the old me would have probably keeled over at the sight of it. And the groceries—don't even get me started on them. The cook in me is disgraced at the utter lack of usage of the kitchen."

"We haven't been the best parents in the last few months, and we see that now more than ever," my dad said, grabbing my leg and holding it up to emphasize. "I don't think your leg has been this small since you were 11 years old," he continued, clear worry in his eyes.

"And that's a problem. We see that that's a problem and we are no longer going to stand idly by. Every day, we wish that we could go back in time and stop Carrie before it was too late. Every day, we curse ourselves for being so wrapped up in our careers and promotions that we were unable to detect something that was killing our daughter. If only we'd have gotten her help, it would be easier to live with ourselves." My dad's eyes were shining with tears, but his grip on my hand remained tight.

"We're not sure why this has happened to you, too," my mother continued, stroking the side of my face. "But this time we're prepared to approach it differently. This time we want to know why. We need answers. We're ready to take on whatever challenges you throw our way and ready to overcome them together. So even though we made a huge mistake by missing that you've been going through something so personal and terrible these last few months, we're hoping that you will allow us to make it up to you."

My heart skipped a beat. These were the words that I needed to hear for so long. Part of me wanted to turn them away, just as they'd done to me, but I couldn't. I remembered the pain I felt when my mother had mistaken me for Carrie, the anger I'd felt when she ignored me and ran away to her room like always, and the misery I'd felt when my father had pretended that everything was fine. I wanted to just get out of bed and run away, leaving them to feel everything I'd felt lately. But I couldn't.

I was so tired and so sick of everything. My immune system felt like it was shutting down. A simple cough could turn into a week-long cold that was annoying, painful, and seemed like it would never go away. Headaches were frequent, and I was almost always dizzy. So even though I wanted to get up and leave, it didn't beat the necessity of my parents. Instead of fighting to get out of their combined embrace, I sank into their arms and accepted it. As much as I wanted to turn them away, I needed them now more than ever. And who was I to reject them? I saw their pain and they saw mine. For once, we were equal in each other's eyes.

Chapter 53

Even though both my parents and I had a lot of healing to do, we definitely became more sensitive to one another after that shared moment. My parents kept me home from school that week. They both knew that I was intelligent and could probably make up most of the work with my eyes closed. However, I'd missed so much school and so many assignments that I was slightly frightened that I may have to repeat the grade and not graduate on time. My parents shunned my fear though, and treated me like a baby for the entire week.

I stayed clothed in warm, fuzzy sweatpants. I'd get up to the go to the bathroom and peek into my father's office. Either he or my mother sat there, typing furiously into the computer. They were almost always researching eating disorders. They'd each joined a support forum, wrote to doctors to ask questions, and investigated rehab centers and healing therapies. Although I didn't want to go to any of those places, I was too tired to voice my opinion or fight back. Instead, I smiled at them weakly and spent most of my time on the couch, watching television.

I felt like I was a child home with the flu. My mother would come to the couch with a small tray filled with chicken noodle soup and toast or crackers, gentle foods that wouldn't upset my stomach. She'd stand there with her hands on her hips and watch me. If I rejected the food, she'd get on her knees, grab the spoon, and direct it into my mouth. I'll admit that it was painful at first to give up everything I'd worked for, but all I could do was remind myself of Carrie.

My mother's transformation was amazing. After that evening, she began showering regularly. She even put on mascara and cheek tint, and her face was no longer paler than a sheet of notebook paper. She bustled around the house with a mop in one hand and a rag in the other. I never knew that the scent of bleach was so comforting. Each morning, she sat outside in her garden and pulled weeds. Although the garden had died without her care, she was slowly reorganizing it into something that could be vibrant again. Sometimes when I passed the window, I could hear her praying or humming. I think that working there and praying was a form of therapy for her. Whenever she came in from tending, she often had a smile on her face, which at first had been unusual to me, but I soon grew happy to see it.

My father was just the same. He often brought me my favorite candy bar home from the office. Slowly, I began to accept his offerings. At first, I rejected them, nearly throwing a tantrum when he brought the candy anywhere near me. But now, I took small squares of it. It was worth it to see the happiness it brought to him and my mom. The research they were doing gave them a sense of how slowly things would progress during my healing, and I feel like they were a little impatient. I think that they wanted to be super-parents and make up for all the time they lost with Carrie, but it wasn't going to happen.

Even though they seemed like entirely new people, I still saw despondent moments within each of them. My mother still retreated to her room sometimes and stared at the wall in silence. My father would sit in his office, spinning a pen in his finger for hours without ever focusing his eyes or doing any real work. I knew that we all had a lot to get through, but there was relief in knowing that we were all doing it together.

To my surprise, my parents had called Andrew and told him the whole story. Like me, he was incredibly angry that he'd been lied to, but he was also extremely worried about me. He offered to fly home and be there to support me, which I thought was very sweet. I assured him it wasn't necessary and promised him that I would take care of myself. While I wasn't sure I could do that right away, I was determined to make it a reality.

Sometimes I woke up and it seemed weird to me that things had changed so quickly. Even though it was hard to let go of the lifestyle

I'd grown accustomed to, there was a fighting power within me that wasn't there before. Sure, there was a struggle between me and the girl inside of me who wanted nothing more than to be skinny, but I had finally realized that the flame of desire within me had burned out a little.

Had I not found Carrie's true cause of death and realized that same fate was coming after me, I may have still been intently dieting. I was incredulous that after reading the documents I was able to see an entirely different body in the mirror, but I also attributed it to some sort of spiritual connection with my twin.

Chapter 54

Days passed without meaning. Most of the time, I lazed in bed staring at the ceiling, feeling lightheaded and sometimes struggling to breathe. My eating was gradual, but at least it was happening. Every time I wanted to give up, I thought of Carrie, and some unexplainable force inside of me made me believe that it was somehow my duty to continue living for her. This time, though, I would not live as her, but in her memory.

I'd decided to remove the mirrors in my room, as hard as that was. I didn't want to see myself because my mind still played tricks on me. There were days when I looked in the mirror and saw a tired, frail skeleton looking back. Other days, my cheeks puffed out just a little too much or my legs seemed like they were packed with fat. I knew it was trickery, though, and eventually decided that in order to survive without conflict, it was necessary to heal without them. I could imagine that I was beautiful without actually forcing myself to look. And yes, that's definitely as hard as it sounds.

Although my parents were somewhat lenient now, I knew they were planning to take me somewhere else. It's amazing how much you can hear through the walls when there's actually communication going on in the house.

For the past few nights, I'd heard my mother fretting over what was going to happen to me. They talked about rehabilitation centers and hospitals, but my mother was frightened at the concept of sending me away. Fiercely, she told my father that she wasn't going to lose my trust again. My dad agreed with her, and the conversation would turn to therapy. Then they'd start talking about putting me on a certain diet and having weekly weigh-ins.

It was all exhausting to me, and I could only listen for so long before closing my eyes and falling asleep again. It seemed that all I did was sleep. I knew that not eating was making me weak, and I honestly tried as hard as I could to stomach what they gave me, but I was torn between the will to live and the repulsion my body expressed at the food. A few times I had the urge to run to the bathroom and purge. I'd give anything to feel that control over my body again, but my parents had started to accompany me to the bathroom, standing outside and listening to make sure I wasn't ridding myself of anything. Unfortunately, I had regressed somewhat, and I knew it would take a lot for them to be able to trust that I could be self-sufficient again.

I can't deny that some of my time wasn't spent thinking of Julian. He was such a significant part of my life, and to lose both him and Carrie hurt beyond belief. Most nights, I would bring my knees up to my chest and squeeze so that the aching pains in my stomach would go away. I'd replay one of our happiest moments together over and over.

It had been a freezing day in January. I had woken up to snow before my alarm went off. Ignoring the icy feeling of the floor beneath my feet and the chill that hit me the second I flung the blanket aside, I raced to the window and placed my hand on it as though I couldn't believe the snow was real. Carrie groaned and covered her head with a pillow, begging me to stop making so much noise. She would soon be disturbed by my father though, who had dramatically swept into the room and began singing, "Snow day," in his impression of Elvis. Carrie opened one eye, yawned, told my father to get out, and burrowed deeper into the blankets. "There are doughnuts," he'd tempted her, and she threw the pillow off the bed and hopped up.

It was odd thinking that at one point in her life, she ran to food. We all bounded down the stairs and slid into our chairs, greeted by warm mugs of cocoa with cinnamon sticks and a plate arranged with orange slices and fresh, hot doughnuts. Andrew, Carrie, and I all grabbed for the food as though we hadn't eaten in months, and we all ate in silence, chewing contentedly as we gazed out the window at the sparkles that were forming a pile of soft, fluffy snow.

The phone rang and Carrie leapt up to get it, probably assuming that it was going to be Jennifer or Peter. The moment she answered, her expression changed to a sour one and she held the phone out, sighing, "Felicia, it's for you," in a bored tone as if it were a huge inconvenience for her to answer my call. I smiled and my face reddened, knowing that it could only be Julian. Andrew snickered and my dad put my arm around my mother's shoulders, and smiled knowingly.

I took the phone into the living room and kicked back on the couch, making sure I could still see the beauty outside.

"Hey," Julian said, his deep voice comforting and melting into warmth on such a chilly day. "Get ready, I'm coming."

That was it. He gave no details or even bothered to wait for my response before hanging up. I'd been on plenty of adventures with Julian before, so I wasn't really uneasy about it. I raced upstairs and pulled on a pair of long-johns, sweatpants, a hooded sweatshirt, a jacket, hat, scarf, and mittens. Just as I was tugging my boots on, the doorbell rang.

"I'll get it!" I cried, flying down the stairs so I could answer the door before any of my family members embarrassed me.

"Hey," I said, out of breath as I yanked the door open.

He didn't speak, but simply grabbed my glove and pulled me out of the house. We started walking north and I suddenly knew we were going. By the time we reached the park, a full-fledged war was already in order. We quickly started rolling snowballs and joined the other kids behind a wall of snow, throwing them with ease. We'd had lots of practice. After a victory, we walked across the street to a little café and bought hot chocolates, warming our hands.

His cheeks had looked rosier than ever, and the stark contrast of the snow and his pale skin against his inky hair was magnificent. Still, I was sure I was just one of the guys and we were just having fun. I pushed any thoughts of romance out of my head and we started the long trek home. It was easy to walk with him. Talking wasn't a problem, but if we remained silent, it wasn't awkward. When I stopped to stick my tongue out to try to catch a snowflake, I lost my balance and fell backwards, but instead of catching me, Julian took the opportunity to tackle me.

"Hey!" I cried, caught completely off-guard. I responded by promptly stuffing snow down the back of his shirt. We messed with each other for a while, throwing snow at back and forth and laughing so hard we could barely breathe. After a few minutes, we lay back on the snow and made snow angels.

The sky was beginning to get dark, and stars twinkled above us, a beautiful accompaniment to the clouds of glitter that dotted our cheeks and clothes. He turned his head to the side and looked at me, and we both smiled at each other shyly. He reached over and grabbed my hand, but only for a second before releasing it and covering up his embarrassment by tossing a snowball in my face. I shrieked and wrestled him to the ground again, but the magical moment had been broken.

Even though nothing physical happened between us that day, it was still my fondest memory of him. It was hard for me to understand how two people could go from talking to and seeing each other every day to having no contact whatsoever. I knew it was my fault, and I could literally feel my chest constricting when I thought of the pain on his face as I repeatedly turned him away. Though I tried to fall asleep replaying the snow day scene, I'd often battle between that and visions of Julian and Locker Girl, which would lead me to have nightmares. I knew it was all silly to think about, but since I couldn't have him in real life, at least I could have in my dreams.

Chapter 55

Soon, the therapy sessions started. Every day, a woman came to my house and talked to me about my eating disorder. I now had the ability to admit that I had one. My parents had requested all of my schoolwork and had begun to teach me at home. Both of them were incredibly intelligent, so I wasn't worried about my grades slipping.

It was hard to get used to the therapist, though. She was young and pretty, and her name was Sasha. She was thin, but not painfully thin, and her hair was flaxen, almost as pale as her icy blue eyes. She was warm and honest, and she made me feel comfortable, especially since she used to have body issues as well. Still, it was hard to get used to someone constantly interrogating me.

She got me to admit to other things too. I admitted that I'd always felt only adequate next to Carrie and that I thought my parents loved her more. I admitted that even though I desperately wanted to be Carrie, I was miserable hanging with her crowd and actually wanted nothing to do with them. And finally, the most annoying thing she got me to admit was that I did have romantic feelings for Julian. The sessions were hard and often heart-wrenching, but it was incredible to discover that I had so much inside of me that I spent so long trying to keep down. It was a relief and a burden at the same time.

Sometimes I got angry with the things Sasha was saying, and other times I wouldn't even answer her. I had somehow morphed into this cold, distant person who was detached from the world around her. As much as I yearned to be back in school, applying for college and doing what everyone else was during senior year, I also was afraid to throw myself back into reality. I missed the scent of fresh pages in a book, the loud chatter in the hallway. I even found myself missing the weird lime gelatin cups.

Whenever I got a craving for food, or I had a positive thought about it, I was supposed to record it in a journal. It was interesting writing a food journal again, because this time, it had to contain a certain amount of calories and the pages were covered in a lot more ink than they ever were before. Although my diet was to increase gradually, I was given gentle, neutral foods so that my stomach wouldn't immediately reject them. It was getting to the point where it became easy to stomach fruits and vegetables, and I also enjoyed drinking soup broth. That initial fear in eating came every time, but it vanished quicker than it ever had before.

I suppose things were shaping up for me, although I was very moody. One day I could be extremely positive and want to take walks outside. Other days, all I wanted to do was lie in bed and stare at the ceiling. Sasha said that it was normal, and that I would get out of my funk in time, but the inconsistency drove me nuts most days. I didn't even understand how I'd gotten to this state. As hard as it was, I'd started clearing the room of some of Carrie's things, which was both a burden and therapeutic at the same time. It was a little easier not seeing her tiny little clothes and thinking that I had to keep attempting to fit in them, but it also broke my heart to see things that I was so familiar with leaving the room.

I still talked to Carrie daily. Sometimes I was angry at her that she'd hid something so crucial from us, and sometimes I was angry at myself for not noticing. See, Carrie was very good at hiding her illness. She somehow managed to look magnificent and possess an ethereal beauty without looking as though she were dying. Thinking back, though, I know that she did look too thin, but there was something so enchanting about her that it was difficult to detect as disease. Sometimes at night, I felt a soft flutter on my forehead, and even though it scared me at first, I now liked to think that it was Carrie laying a hand on my head, letting me know that she was with me through this struggle.

Chapter 56

As the weather got warmer, I often helped my mother in her garden. I now understood how nice it was to be working under the sun, smelling the fresh herbs and feeling like you had some kind of connection to nature. We'd gone to the hardware store and picked out seeds, and the garden was soon blooming with fresh tomatoes, cucumbers, lettuce, carrots, peppers, cilantro, and even small potatoes. We'd also planted lots of herbs and edible flowers, and in honor of Carrie, started a new strawberry patch. It amazed me how much easier it was to eat food that I'd grown myself. I soon became fascinated with the process of growing the vegetables, and I'd sit with my mother in the kitchen as she'd pull out a dusty cookbook from her mother and make soups, roasts, and salads, and I was surprised that I found myself eager to eat them.

I'd started to put on weight. Although it was unsettling at first, each day I felt stronger. Muscles were slowly emerging, and instead of feeling sick, I began to feel healthier. A typical day for me included taking vitamins and eating a breakfast of fruit, whole-grain toast with peanut butter, and orange juice. Then I'd garden and come and help my mother make a fresh salad for lunch. Later, I'd ride my bike or take a walk with my dad, and then we'd all eat a light meal of soup or roasted vegetables. In the evening, I would study, read, and I'd even pulled my old keyboard out of the attic and had started writing music again.

I couldn't believe how much I could change in such a short time, but I was proud of myself. So proud, in fact, that I allowed myself to be weighed and even glanced in a mirror without having a breakdown.

My face was mostly clear, and my time in the garden had brought a healthier tint of color to my face. My mom had started blending herbs with avocados and lemons to make a homemade shampoo which was supposedly strengthening my follicles, and although my hair was still thin, it was looking a little better every day. I suppose the best part was seeing that my cheeks no longer looked so sunken in. My eyes were a little less tired, and everything looked just a tiny bit brighter. Every day, my mother told me I was beautiful.

Starting to eat was definitely a process. We took it a little at a time, and some days I had to force myself to eat, because my parents were looking at me with such encouragement and hope in their eyes that I felt guilty if I didn't. Soon though, I was doing it for me, too. At first, I must have chewed my food at least thirty times before I allowed myself to swallow, because the texture, taste, and smell of it made me nauseous. As time passed, I realized that my body felt infinitely better when I'd eaten. It was easier to do homework, I could stay awake for longer periods of times, and somehow, it was a little easier to offer up a smile or two as days passed.

It was refreshing to live in a clean home again. Sometimes, we'd open up the windows and let the sunlight in, and we'd play oldies and work on different rooms and join each other for lunch after. It was weird getting used to my parents acting normal again, but we soon fell into a routine that felt as natural as it had before.

I wrote enough papers, solved enough formulas, and did enough science experiments that it was determined that I was caught up on work and would be able to return to school for the last month. I wasn't sure if I wanted to, but I thought of Carrie, and how she wouldn't be able to have her graduation. I didn't mistake my wanting to go back to school as living as Carrie, but rather living some of my life in honor of her.

Chapter 57

Sasha questioned me extensively to make sure I was ready to go back, and sometimes, I wasn't sure that I was. She gave me tips on talking to people, almost like she was training me to socialize or telling me how to reenter the world. I hadn't thought I'd been gone for that long. I'd learned how unnecessary it was to compare my body to other bodies, as everyone was constantly developing in different ways and the world held different standards of beauty and yada, yada, yada.

I liked Sasha, but some of the things she said just sounded made-up to me. I wasn't so far gone that I'd have a breakdown if I went back to school, but I did know that I was going to focus on my work, ignore the people that made me feel bad about myself, and reward myself for working hard and believing that I could get through this and achieve my goals. At least, that's the mantra Sasha made me repeat.

As nice as it was to be home and not have to deal with Allison or Jennifer or seeing Julian and Locker Girl, I also knew that if I didn't throw myself into reality, I might never go back. I was tired of staring at the ceilings every night, and as my body grew stronger, I willed my brain to as well. The night before I was to go back, my mom prepared a special dinner, and we all ate as a family.

She'd set the table with pretty flowered plates that had been favorites of Carrie's. Dinner consisted of one of my old favorite meals: taco salad. The salad started with fresh romaine lettuce. Then we added black beans, red onion, cilantro, avocado, Monterey jack and cheddar cheese, corn, tomatoes, and grilled chicken breast. The salad was tossed with a spicy Texas ranch dressing and garnished with tortilla strips. It was wonderful to be able to add some of our own plants this year, and I'd even had enough courage to eat the cheese. The old me would have turned it away simply for its calories. My father set a pitcher of lemonade with swirling strawberry, orange, and lime slices in it. Our little fiesta was actually very heartwarming, and I found myself thankful that my parents had pushed so hard for me to get better.

Like any concerned parents, they were worried about a relapse. Since they wanted to consistently monitor me, they never sent me away to an actual rehabilitation center, and they were hoping they'd never have to. Armed with all of their research and tips from Sasha, they often repeated facts and statistics to me and made me aware that they'd always be watching. I felt slightly babied, but I also knew how much they cared, and knew that we all had to earn each other's trust back, so I allowed them to do whatever was necessary.

As the evening drew to a close, I sat in my room, my nerves jumbling around my stomach. I reached into my closet and fingered one of Carrie's old sweaters, feeling the softness and closing my eyes just for a minute to remember what she'd looked like in it. Beautiful, I remembered, but it also was something that I really didn't find appealing for myself. I reminded myself that I needed to start living independently and thoughtfully, so I glanced over to my side of the closet and found one of my favorite old outfits.

It was an outfit I wore to outings, parties, and when I wanted to feel my best and most confident. I pulled out black tights, silver-studded motorcycle boots, a floral patterned mini-dress, a wide, buckled belt, and a black fedora hat. The look had always been completed with my homemade feather earrings and matching necklace. While it wasn't something Jennifer or her followers would be caught dead in, it was something that I thought looked beautiful, and I felt strong and like myself when I was wearing it. I remembered that I had never cared what they thought before, and I shouldn't care now.

Giddy and somewhat sick all at the same time, I climbed into bed. As Sasha had instructed me to do, I went over what I'd eaten in the day and how I could improve that list tomorrow. I realized that for the first time in weeks, my list matched almost exactly what she recommended. I felt proud of myself, and for once, I wasn't desperate to get rid of the fullness in my stomach. Instead, I just felt good. Next, I spent some time praying. It was hard to do sometimes, as I was often angry for losing Carrie, but it was also sort of a coping method. I wasn't necessarily praying to anyone in particular, but just voicing my thoughts gave me some relief. Lastly, I spoke directly to Carrie, asking her for guidance on such an important day.

"Carrie, I miss you," I whispered aloud, a lone tear tricking down my cheek. "I would give anything to have you by my side tomorrow. I remember when we were little and everything was easy, when the biggest worry we had was which teacher we were going to trick tomorrow by wearing the same clothing. I remember long talks with you, dreaming about weddings, and talking about moving out together someday. Even though none of that can happen now, I want you to know that I'll never forget it. I want you to know that if I could go back in time, I'd do whatever I could to make you feel beautiful, to help you remember how special you were to everyone. You were beautiful, probably the most beautiful girl I've ever seen.

And even though that sounds biased," I laughed through my tears, "we didn't look exactly alike, and there was something about you that made you similar to a princess in a fairy tale. Please, help me to get through tomorrow. I know you're watching over me, and I don't know how I'm going to make it through this life without you, but I want you to know that I'm not giving up this time. I was so close to losing it and didn't realize how lucky I was to still have life. This time, I'm doing it for the both of us. You'll be in my heart forever, sister," I finished, bringing my fingers to my lips and then my heart. I sobbed myself to sleep that night, but realized I was happier than I'd been in a long time.

Chapter 58

I woke up before my alarm went off. I could smell coffee brewing downstairs and knew that my parents had woken up early to prepare breakfast for such a special day. I trudged downstairs, trying to ignore how hard my heart was beating and pulled out the chair.

"Morning, honey," my dad said, setting a plate of my mother's homemade granola in front of me. Next to that was a slice of whole-grain toast and red grapefruit.

"Thanks," I mumbled, drinking some orange juice and eating as much of the breakfast that my stomach would allow. My parents didn't ask too many questions, and we ate contentedly.

After, I ran upstairs and hopped in the shower, using the nutrient-rich shampoo and running my hands through hair that seemed to be growing thicker every day. When I was finished, I rubbed some moisturizer on my skin and applied some light makeup, taking care so that my face didn't look sickly or washed out. I didn't copy Carrie's makeup, but stuck to an old routine I used to use quite often.

I brushed some brown eye shadow on to highlight the blue in my eyes and ran a mascara wand through my lashes a couple times. A light dusting of peach blush and a swipe of lip gloss and I was finished. I dressed in the outfit I'd chosen the night before and scrunched my hair up so that it came out long and wavy. Tilting the hat at just the right angle on my head, I looked in the mirror and felt pretty for the first time in ages. I saw a part of Carrie in me, but most importantly, I saw Felicia, someone I hadn't seen in a long time.

I smiled genuinely at my reflection and picked up my backpack, ready not only to face my demons, but to start my life again.

My parents were waiting outside for me, and as I climbed into the car, the queasy feeling in my stomach returned. Ever since the accident, I'd been wary of getting in cars, but I reminded myself that my dad was a safe driver and that I couldn't be scared of things forever. The drive to school was short, and each of my parents kissed my cheek and assured me that they would drop everything to come get me if I found it necessary. I thanked them, took a deep breath, and got out of the car.

As I wandered into the building, some students stared, as I'd prepared myself for. A few of them, even Martha, offered me smiles, and I smiled back at them tentatively. My teachers were warm in their greetings, and in my first few classes, I'd realized that the preparation I'd been doing at home had actually put me ahead of what we were learning now.

When I passed Jennifer and Allison in the hall, the two ignored me, save for a brief glance in my direction, but in my opinion, being ignored was much better than being taunted. My day had been going so well so far that I was almost giddy. In the cafeteria, I'd eaten a small salad, half a grilled cheese sandwich, and even managed to snag a lime gelatin cup. Martha invited me to sit with her, and she was careful not to reference my eating disorder, even though Sasha had encouraged me to talk about it. Instead, we discussed a book being read in the Honors English class.

I glanced towards Julian's table, but he wasn't there. Interestingly enough, I saw Locker Girl sitting with a boy in our grade named Devon. He was in a grunge band, had a short ponytail, and chiseled, model-like features. He was well-known for his soulful lyrics and pouty lips, and she seemed to be gazing at him with admiration. My heart skipped a beat, and I felt satisfaction seeing the two together, but I was still disappointed that I hadn't seen Julian. I wasn't sure when I'd be able to apologize to him, or if I'd ever be able to talk to him again, but I knew that seeing his familiar face would be comfort enough.

The rest of the day went by quickly but successfully. I couldn't believe how strong I felt. Lots of people told me that I looked great, and the work we were doing in class was so easy that I knew I'd have spare time to play piano tonight. In that moment, I felt so grateful for my parents and Sasha, and I knew in my heart that Carrie had played a role in my healing. The way I felt now was almost better than how I'd felt before I'd stopped eating. I knew now that I'd never go back to dieting again—the hardship it brought upon my body was not worth it.

There was only one thing missing from my day of happiness, and that was Julian. Assuming he was absent, I shrugged and decided I'd spend the night dreaming up ways to apologize or maybe stick a note in his locker or something. I was ashamed at the way I'd acted, and I realized that a life without him as my best friend was one that was very lonely and somewhat meaningless. I mused over the various ways to reunite with him as I fished books out of my locker that needed to be taken home for homework. One book was caught in the corner of the locker, and as I yanked it out, I flew backwards. If anything were representative of the fact that I was back, it had to be my clumsiness, my bizarrely frequent crashes.

"Oof!" I groaned, feeling my body bang against someone's shoulder. An arm swiftly reached down and set me upright.

I gazed into eyes I'd been dreaming of.

"Hey," he said, his eyes crinkling up at the corners and an amused smile playing on his face.

I could almost hear Carrie laughing at me from above. My klutziness had finally led me to the right place. I'd fallen directly into Julian's arms.

Purchase other Black Rose Writing titles at and use promo code PRINT to receive a 20% discount.

CPSIA information can be obtained at www.ICGtesting.com
Printed in the USA
LVOW09s1108241014

410351LV00003B/283/P